Ahead of them stars twinkled and glittered like diamonds tossed onto a black velvet quilt. Nick kept his grip on Shay's hand, just to make sure she was okay.

In truth, standing there with her, sharing this moment made his own breathing uneven. Beautiful Shay, so near he wanted to draw her into the protection of his arms, and ensure she knew she never had to fear again. But that would betray her trust in him. Besides, though he was her friend, he had no future to offer this wonderful woman.

Nothing more than friendship.

"Our star show is starting. See that?" She pointed upward, tracking a meteor as it flew across the sky. "And that. It's like God is lighting the sky especially for us." Shay's eyes blazed with excitement.

She tilted her head sideways to rest it on his shoulder for a brief moment before she stepped away. "You're the best friend I ever had, Nick."

LOIS RICHER

began her travels the day she read her first book and realized that fiction provided an extraordinary adventure. Creating that adventure for others became her obsession. With millions of books in print, Lois continues to enjoy creating stories of joy and hope. She and her husband love to travel, which makes it easy to find the perfect setting for her next story. Lois would love to hear from you via www.loisricher.com, loisricher@yahoo.com or on Facebook.

Perfectly Matched
Lois Richer

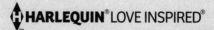
HARLEQUIN® LOVE INSPIRED®

Recycling programs
for this product may
not exist in your area.

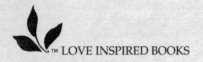

™ LOVE INSPIRED BOOKS

ISBN-13: 978-0-373-87799-7

PERFECTLY MATCHED

Copyright © 2013 by Lois M. Richer

www.LoveInspiredBooks.com

Printed in U.S.A.

Who then can ever keep Christ's love from us?
When we have trouble or calamity,
when we are hunted down or destroyed, is it
because He doesn't love us anymore? And if we
are hungry, or penniless, or in danger, or
threatened with death, has God deserted us? No.
—*Romans* 8:35

Chapter One

"I hurt, Uncle Nick."

"Aw, I'm sorry, sweetheart." Nick Green tenderly shifted the weight of the little girl clinging to his neck as he stepped into the hospital hallway. "Is that better, honey?"

Maggie sighed and laid her head on his shoulder. "It's okay."

It was so *not* okay that a five-year-old accepted pain as part of her world. A blaze of anger seared his insides, quickly joined by uselessness and frustration. One drunken driver had inflicted so much pain on Nick's family, leaving Maggie bereft of her parents and physically damaged. Not only had she sustained a host of internal injuries, but her legs had also been crushed in the accident. She'd endured many surgeries but she still couldn't walk.

"You did very well with the doctors, darlin'," he encouraged. "Now let's go get some ice cream." He needed it, to wash away the aftertaste of their unappetizing hospital lunch.

"Nick?" A voice with faint vestiges of an English accent made him stop.

"Yeah?" He turned around and blinked at the woman striding down the hall toward him. The hair gave her away—a glorious tumble of copper-colored waves and curls. But if the hair hadn't done it, the famous emerald-green eyes in that heart-shaped face would have. He grinned. "Shay Parker's back in town."

"I always told you I would be back. But what are *you* doing here in Hope?" Shay tapped him playfully against the chest, her smile dazzling him. "You insisted Seattle was your home, yet here you are in New Mexico, and with such a beautiful lady." Shay touched a finger to the end of the little girl's tipped-up nose. "Who is this?"

"This is my niece, Magdalena. We call her Maggie."

"Hello, Maggie. I'm Shay." She held out a slender hand for the child to shake.

"Hi." Maggie kept her hands tucked around Nick's neck. But she did risk a smile before shyly pressing her head into her uncle's shoulder.

"Maggie and I are going for ice cream," Nick explained. "Want to join us?"

He knew she would. For as long as he'd known Shay, she'd never been able to resist ice cream. They'd met when they were twelve, the year she'd moved with her dad from England. When their friend Jessica had died, their shared grief had turned into a close friendship. Taller than most of their classmates, they'd played basketball, picked pecans on her grandfather's farm and gone together to their senior prom. Shay had become an ardent supporter of Nick's football prowess, and she'd actually encouraged his love of inventing and tinkering with machines while most of their peers scoffed.

And yet, as Nick studied her now, he realized he'd never fully appreciated her exquisite beauty. Pretty stupid considering Shay Parker had gone on to become a world-class model.

"I'd love some ice cream, Nick. I can hardly wait to get out of this place." Shay glanced down the hospital hallway and faked a shudder.

"Us either. But why you?" Curious, Nick walked outside beside her.

"I need a break. I've been jumping through hoops to get privileges at this hospital," she joked, touching the unblemished skin at her throat. "They act like physiotherapists are criminals."

"It's probably a security thing. I imagine they're trying to be extra careful given the number of people the new mine is drawing into town." Nick stopped at his truck, which was sheltered under a huge mesquite tree, the only one in the lot that had already bloomed. He'd managed to snag this shady spot by arriving for Maggie's appointment with the traveling neurologist before sunrise. "Want to ride with us?" He glanced around. "I don't see that red dream-mobile you always talked about owning," he teased. "Change your mind about getting a convertible?"

"I think I'm beginning to. My car is in the shop. Again. So, yeah, a ride would be great." Shay paused a moment to study the splashes of green dotting the desert landscape. "Don't you just love the desert in spring?"

"April's nice, yeah." Nick paused a second to look around then focused on fastening Maggie into her booster seat before he held the front door open for Shay.

"It's wonderful to walk around Hope freely, not like in the big city where you have to be on guard all the time," she murmured, glancing around the parking lot.

Nick frowned. If Shay felt so safe here, why was she looking over her shoulder like that?

But then he remembered. Three years ago he'd been in New York for a meeting with his agent and decided to pay Shay a surprise visit. Confused by her haunted look and nervous manner, Nick had been stunned when she'd confessed that she was being stalked. His temper still blazed at the memory of her trembling tone as she related what she'd gone through. Her stalker had her private number, knew where she lived and had not only snuck onto her set and left gifts for her there, but gloated that he'd even touched her several times without her noticing.

Nick figured Shay's lack of success with the police meant that either they didn't believe her or they'd given up. So, in Nick's mind, it was up to him to help Shay, just as he would have helped one of his sisters. He'd hung around after they'd had lunch, hoping her stalker would call again. Nick figured the guy liked taking chances and probably felt that no one would discover his identity now that the police had given up. No doubt he enjoyed terrifying Shay, making her feel helpless. That infuriated Nick. When the call came, Nick put a lid on his own reactions to the creep's mockery of Shay's vulnerability. Anger still surged at the memory of that snide and gloating voice exulting in the death of Shay's father.

When the guy boasted that Shay now had no one to protect her, Nick saw red. He'd grabbed her phone and told the slimeball Shay had innumerable friends like him waiting en masse to bring down their wrath on his head if he didn't leave Shay alone. Nick also intimated that the police were ready to haul the guy off to jail. The guy hung up fast. After that, he disappeared and wasn't seen again, according to the bodyguard Nick had hired for Shay.

"Earth calling Nick? Hello?" Shay snapped her fingers in front of his face to draw him out of his introspection. "Where were you?"

"Daydreaming." He tweaked Maggie's nose. He'd ask Shay about her stalker later. "What kind of ice cream are we getting, Maggie-mine?"

"Choc'late, Uncle Nick," she told him without hesitation. She peeked up through her lashes.

"I should know that, shouldn't I, after the number of cones I've bought you." As Nick tugged playfully at a hank of her short, dark hair, he noticed Shay's quick scan of the braces encircling his niece's legs. "Privileges must mean you're starting at Whispering Hope Clinic. When?"

"Yesterday. Jaclyn and Brianna have been nagging me to join them for ages." Shay shrugged her elegant shoulders. "So I have."

Nick knew all about the youthful vow Shay, Jaclyn and Brianna had made to build a clinic for kids after Jaclyn's fifteen-year-old twin sister, Jessica, had died. It was their way of honoring her, making sure no other child went without the medical care Jessica had needed. Doctors had been sadly lacking in Hope when they were kids. But now Whispering Hope Clinic was open and, according to Nick's mom, full of activity with Jaclyn as a pediatrician and Brianna as a child psychologist. Now that Shay had joined the clinic as physiotherapist, Nick figured the place would get even busier.

Though Jaclyn and Brianna were married to Nick's friends, Kent McCloy and Zac Enders, Nick knew Shay wasn't married. He'd heard in Seattle that she'd left modeling but he'd only learned several months earlier, at Brianna and Zac's wedding, that Shay had finished her physiotherapy degree a while ago. He'd had very few moments during that busy weekend to discuss her return to Hope, and Shay had left town the next morning. The following weekend Nick had been injured during a game, and his career as a pro quarterback had ended in the blink of an eye. Then had come Maggie's car accident. Life hadn't settled down since.

Nick wondered what had delayed Shay's homecoming till now.

"I heard about your shoulder injury, Nick." Shay's lustrous green eyes lost their twinkle. "I'm so sorry. I know how much you loved football."

"Thanks." Nick did not want to discuss the demoralizing loss of his career as a pro quarterback.

"How long have you been back in Hope?" she asked.

"About a week. Mom's finding it tough to make all the medical trips to Las Cruces with Maggie, so I came to help." He glanced at his niece, unwilling to discuss the accident that had killed his beloved sister Georgia and her husband. Besides, he'd told Shay the important parts when she'd called with her sympathies. Just hearing her soft, quiet voice that morning had helped him get through what followed.

Nick's throat tightened at the loss he hadn't yet fully accepted. How could it be part of God's plan for his sister's car to get hit by a semitruck?

"How's your mom?" Shay adjusted Maggie's braced left legs to a slightly different angle, then smiled at the little girl as if they shared a secret.

"She's okay, though her arthritis is really bad. I had hoped she'd stay with me in Seattle, but she couldn't take the cold or the humidity. She always came back here." He paused, glanced at his niece. "Now Maggie's with her. To Mom, Hope is home."

"To me, too," Shay agreed. She grinned as if the little town offered everything she needed. And maybe it did, for Shay. But for Nick, Hope could be only a temporary stop. He had to get back to the city and begin the coaching job that would allow him to provide for his family now that pro ball was out.

"Want to eat outside?" He pulled into a stall in front of the local general store where the owners still piled cones high with real ice cream. "The sun's burnt off this morning's chill by now."

"Maggie and I will find a place in the park while you get our treats." Without waiting for him, Shay slipped from her seat, quickly unfastened the little girl's restraints and lifted her out.

Nick noticed that Maggie didn't make her usual squeal of pain and felt a rush of guilt. He'd been doing it wrong. Disgust washed over him at the thought that he'd even inadvertently hurt his niece.

"I'll have butter pecan," Shay called as she walked away.

"Still supporting the pecan industry, huh?" he teased.

"Have to." Shay's eyes twinkled as she glanced at him over one shoulder. Gold sparks of mischief lurked in their emerald depths. "I guess you haven't heard. I bought back my grandfather's farm. Support the pecan farmers," she chanted in imitation of a protestor.

Surprise held Nick immobile as Shay chose a grassy spot and set Maggie gently against the smoothed-off trunk of a towering palm tree. A moment later the former model's melodic laughter burst into the sunlit afternoon, her face glowing with happiness and health as she folded her long legs beneath her and settled next to the child.

Nick strode toward the store but jerked to a halt when, for the first time since the accident, he heard Maggie giggle. Choked up by the sound, he hurried inside to buy the ice cream, overwhelmed by the fact that his old friend had made his usually somber niece laugh.

As Nick waited for his order to be filled, he puzzled over Shay's decision to purchase her former home. She was famous—she'd been one of the best-paid models in the world. She'd spent years wearing elegant clothes and expensive makeup—neither of which, in Nick's opinion, she needed to enhance her loveliness. Shay could have bought the nicest house in town. She didn't need to dirty her manicured nails with nuts and soil.

So why buy back the farm?

Nick studied her through the window. The stunning woman now sitting with Maggie seemed worlds apart from the shy, grieving English girl who'd arrived in Hope having just lost her mother. Back then, quiet, reticent Shay had struggled to fit in at school. But Shay had lost that shyness when Jessica, Zac, Kent, Brianna, Jaclyn, Nick and Shay had all become good friends.

Then, in her junior year of high school, Shay's grandfather died. After that, her dad lost the farm. They'd struggled until, on a dare from Brianna and Jaclyn, Shay had entered a contest at a mall in Las Cruces and won a modeling contract in her senior year. Instead of studying physiotherapy to join the clinic she and her friends were going to build to honor Jessica, Shay had opted to model so she could support her father.

Now Shay Parker was back in Hope. It sounded as if she had her future happily mapped out. Nick wished he felt the same. The assistant coaching job his football team had offered him was not the career he'd planned for himself. Shrugging away his disquiet, he muted his concerns about the future, paid for the cones and carried them outside.

"You're having vanilla?" Shay demanded as he handed over the ice cream. She blinked at his nod. "Forty-one flavors and you chose vanilla? Who are you and what have you done with the adventurous, always unexpected Nick Green? Maggie, are you sure this is your uncle?"

The little girl giggled, and Nick marveled at the sound again.

"Well, I'm shocked. The old Nick would have chosen green bananas with licorice or huckleberry with liver pâté—anything but vanilla," Shay teased.

"You know they don't even make those flavors. Anyway, the old Nick is gone." *And been replaced by whom?* Nick asked himself. Shay had given up her career of her own volition, but Nick felt as if his had been stolen from him.

"I'm sorry—I wasn't thinking. Was the surgery successful?" Shay frowned.

"The doctors said it was a total success. Now it only hurts when I move," he joked. Shay didn't laugh. "I can't throw a football fifty feet," he admitted. Her eyes darkened with sympathy that Nick didn't want, so he moved the focus back to her. "Why did you buy the farm, Shay?"

"Because it's my home. I know every nook and cranny of that land, and I always liked living there." She smirked. "I like it even more now. The old house was a wreck, so I had it torn down and built a new one. You should visit me. I've got the best view in this county."

"But surely you don't intend to farm? The orchards must be in very bad shape." Nick couldn't fathom what this model-turned-physiotherapist would do with a pecan farm.

"Well, I was told the harvest in December didn't yield much. But I do think the trees will come back eventually. I'll wait and see. For now I have to concentrate on my practice." Her voice softened. "Anyway, it's not the orchard I wanted, Nick, as much as my home. Dad had big plans for the family place. I'd like to fulfill some of them, but that's down the road. For now, I have to live somewhere, so it might as well be on familiar territory."

Nick searched her face. He knew her well enough to know there was something she wasn't saying. Shay avoided his intent look by tossing the scant remains of her cone in a nearby trash can. She offered Maggie a tissue to clean up her hands then asked, "Would you like to try the swing, honey?"

The little girl frowned, her eyes speculative. Finally she nodded, very slowly.

"I'll help you." Shay lifted his niece into her arms and carried her to the swing. With an ease that surprised Nick, she set Maggie on the seat, told her to hang on then gently pushed until the swing swayed back and forth.

Concern grabbed at Nick as alarm filled Maggie's face.

"Uh, Shay, maybe you shouldn't—"

She pinned him with her world-famous stare. "It's okay, Nick," she assured him, her quiet, firm tone communicating that she had everything under control.

Nick's argument died on his lips. He nodded and she continued pushing Maggie, offering encouragement.

"Can your toes touch the sky, Maggie?" Shay's casual gaze intensified as she assessed the child. "Wow! That's amazing."

Nick sat on the end of a child's slide and observed Shay coax Maggie through a series of moves using little dares that began with "Betcha can't…" Maggie responded every time, engrossed in the tasks as she pushed herself to prove she could do it. After a few minutes Shay slowed the swing, hugged the little girl and said something that widened Maggie's grin. Shay took the swing beside her and together they swayed back and forth, chattering like magpies. Eventually Shay beckoned him over.

"I think Maggie has had enough swinging," she said, tilting her head to indicate Maggie's drooping body.

Nick took his cue, strode forward and bent to lift his niece free. Before he could, Shay reached out and touched his hands, her fingers firm as she rearranged his grip.

"Higher," she murmured in his ear. "Like this. Not under her knees."

So he *had* been hurting Maggie. Inside him, anger exploded at his clumsiness and the seeming hopelessness of her situation. The doctor's words today hadn't been encouraging. Maggie wasn't moving as much as expected. Small wonder. She had missed so many therapy sessions in Las Cruces. It wasn't his mom's fault but—well, at least he was here to help now. If only he could do more.

Using great care, Nick set Maggie in the truck and fastened her seat belt. He waited for Shay to climb inside, but she pushed the door closed.

"I'll walk back. I need the exercise after that gigantic cone." She patted her flat midriff and grinned. "I've gained five pounds since I've been back."

He couldn't see where. Shay looked fantastic in her white

fitted pants and navy blue shirt. Her peaches-and-cream skin, flawless except for the trademark spattering of freckles across her elegant nose, glowed radiant in the unrelenting desert sun.

Nick blinked in surprise as a thud of male appreciation hit him. Shay was gorgeous, of course. Always had been. But he wasn't attracted to her—they'd been friends, that's all.

"Uh, we'd better get—"

"Nick, can you come to my place tonight?" Shay asked quietly. "I need to talk to you about Maggie."

Since that was exactly what he wanted to talk to her about, he nodded. "Seven-thirty?"

She agreed. "Good seeing you, Nick." Shay lifted her hand and almost touched his arm before she quickly backed away.

"Good to see you, too, Shay," he said, confused by her abrupt actions, almost as if she were afraid of the contact. "I'll see you later."

As he drove away, he glanced in the rearview mirror. Shay stood where he'd left her, staring after them, copper hair glistening, her lovely face pensive.

"Is Shay your girlfriend, Uncle Nick?"

"Huh? No." Nick laughed. That was absurd, of course. Nick didn't do relationships—well, not with the memory of his father's abandonment melded into his brain. The entire town had gossiped and mourned Cal Green's lack of consideration for his family. When his father had finally walked out for good, Nick had heard enough whispers and pity to last a lifetime. He'd tried once to rebuild his connection with his father and twice to have a romantic relationship and he'd failed badly at all three. Fearing he might take after his father, Nick now avoided those kinds of emotional entanglements.

"Then how come you know her?" Maggie asked.

"Shay's a friend. We grew up together."

"I like her," Maggie said while yawning. She closed her eyes and drifted to sleep as he drove home.

But Nick was wide awake. And foremost on his mind was why Shay hadn't mentioned anything about their encounter in New York. Maybe he'd ask her about that tonight.

He looked again in his mirror and saw her walking across the park, her pace furious.

As if she was running away from something.

Or someone.

Yes, Shay Parker was most definitely not telling him something.

Chapter Two

Shay checked her yard for the third time in less than five minutes, sat down to knit, then rose and peered through the window again, anxious to determine what had caused the crunching sound on the gravel driveway.

Nothing there.

She inhaled and counted to ten while fighting back the burgeoning cloud of alarm now swelling inside her head. This was what no one understood, what she'd only recently learned for herself. Her panic attacks were about losing control. That's what her stalker had left her with—the fear that her world would go careening out of control and that she'd unravel worse than she ever had before.

And there would be nobody there to help her put herself back together again.

Think about Nick, she ordered her jittery brain. Nick was a friend, a very good friend.

Had been a friend, her brain corrected without her permission. Because if he was a friend, why, when Nick's fingers had brushed hers when he'd handed her the cone, had she felt fear? Sure, she'd covered by making a joke about his ice cream choice, but later when she'd almost touched his arm, her pulse had skittered and she'd jerked away because she'd had a flashback.

Her stalker's name was Dom. Or at least, that's what he'd called himself. He'd said he touched her, and she hadn't known.

The memory of someone brushing her shoulder and touching her arm before a shoot still haunted her. Back then Shay hadn't suspected anything untoward, not until she'd received that phone call—*I'm closer than you think. I can touch you whenever I want. In fact, I already have, lots of times.* Almost three years later and she still hadn't rid herself of the panic. That's what had ruined her relationship with Eric. What man wanted to be with someone who froze like a nervous Nellie whenever he embraced her?

Eric had taught Shay that she could never have a normal relationship with a man. The shame, the embarrassment and, most of all, the longing to love haunted her still.

"Shay?"

Shay yelped as she jerked back to awareness. An involuntary rush of fear clutched her throat until she realized Nick stood outside her door.

"Uh, can I come in?" He rattled the handle, studying her with a quizzical look.

"Yes. Of course. Sure. Come on in." She flushed as she unlatched the two locks and pushed open the door. "Sorry. I was woolgathering."

He frowned when she flicked both locks back into place once he was inside.

"You're expecting pecan robbers or something?" he joked. "Not that you shouldn't take precautions," he added when she frowned at him. His gaze followed her motions as she checked and rechecked the two very solid locks.

"Can't be too careful." Embarrassed that he'd noticed her obsessive security measures, Shay regrouped, led the way into her living room and waved a hand. "Have a seat, Nick. Iced tea or coffee?"

"Whatever you have is fine. Um—" Nick eyed the furniture and remained standing.

Shay suddenly realized all the seats were covered with skeins of wool she'd sorted earlier. "Oh. Sorry."

He remained silent while she scooped her yarn, needles and a pattern book from the biggest, roomiest chair. Then he said, "That looks complicated."

"It's going to be a blanket for Jaclyn's baby. I just hope I can get it finished before she delivers." Shay set the project in a woven basket on the floor next to the chair facing her wall of windows. "There. Now you can sit down."

"Why did you pick something so difficult to make?" he asked.

"If it was easy, it wouldn't be much of a gift," she said with a quick smile. "I want my gift for this baby to be as special as Jaclyn is to me. I'll be right back."

When she returned with a tray that had two drinks and a dish of tortilla chips and salsa, he said, "You weren't kidding about your view, were you? The orchards don't look bad from here."

"I hired someone to prune things a bit." She sat down, aware of his wide-eyed scrutiny of her home.

"Maybe you should hire the same guy to cut all that tall grass in your backyard," Nick suggested. "The rains in January spurred a lot of growth, but now it's so dry that if a wildfire starts, that grass will feed it like gas. Your house could be in jeopardy."

"I'll get it done," she promised, and added "soon" when he kept staring at her.

"Good." Nick's bemused gaze took in the splashes of color on the walls, the floors and the furniture. "This sure isn't what I expected your place would look like."

"What did you expect? Steel and glass and leather? Glitz and glamour?" Shay burst out laughing at his nod. "But, Nick, that's not me."

"Are you kidding?" He scowled. "How is glitz and glamour not you?"

"That's what I did," she said gently. "That's how I made my living." She pointed to the wall opposite them. "That's the real me."

"You made this?" Nick got up to examine an intricately stitched design of a little girl paddling at the seashore. It could have been Shay once, a long time ago. "It's very nice. But—"

"Being a model only looks glamorous, Nick. There's actually a lot of downtime, waiting for the photographer or the makeup person or hairstylist, and more endless hours in airports. Dad encouraged me to do handwork to pass the time. When I finished something, I'd put it away in a box he gave me." She was *not* going to call it a hope chest. "That's it there."

Nick knelt in front of the intricately decorated trunk. "It's lovely."

"I kept putting things in there because I knew one day I'd have my own place, a place I could make into my home." She waved a hand. "Most of what you see here is stuff I've made."

Nick rose, examined cushions, hangings and the little stool she'd re-covered with a tapestry she told him she'd found in Italy.

"Did you make this, too?" he asked, indicating a canvas dotted with handprints that took up the entire wall behind the dining table.

"No. That was a gift from the kids I worked with before I came here." As always, the colorful finger-painted mural made her smile. "I have the other half of it hanging in my office." Shay waited for him to sit down again, sipping her drink as she puzzled over how to broach the subject she'd been musing on since she'd met with Maggie's medical team earlier. "Catch me up on your world, Nick."

"Not much to tell since we talked after Maggie's accident." He returned to his seat and took a drink before he spoke, his voice flat and emotionless. "Tore my shoulder, had surgery, gave up pro ball."

"And now?" she prodded. "I know some athletes go into broadcasting. Is that what you'll do?"

"No. I'm lousy at that. I get too caught up in the game and forget to make the comments they want. The only thing I know is playing football." Nick's face tightened into tense lines. His brown eyes deepened to that dark shade that told her he was brooding over something.

"You know a lot more than football, Nick." Shay could see him mentally reject that but she let it hang, waiting.

"It seems I don't know much that makes me employable. Anyway, I have six months' leave and then I'll go back to the team. They've offered me a job with the coaching staff." Nick sounded—discouraged?

"Six months is lots of time," she told him optimistically. "I'm sure you'll be all healed up by then."

"Oh, I'm healthy now. I asked for the six months so I could help Mom with Maggie, but I have to go back then for sure." His response sounded less than thrilled.

"Well, a job is good. Isn't it?" Shay added when he got lost in his thoughts.

"Yeah, a job is very good. Only I don't like the thought of leaving Mom here, alone, to manage with Maggie," Nick admitted. "It's a lot for her to take on a kid Maggie's age. Mom did so much for us, raising all of us on her own. She deserves to have some time for herself."

"Knowing your mother's great big heart, I seriously doubt she feels that way." Shay sipped her tea and made a mental note to talk to Mrs. Green about her arthritis. But first she had to deal with the past. "I need to say something to you, Nick."

"Go ahead." He leaned back and waited.

"I—uh, never did thank you properly for your help in New York." She swallowed hard and forced herself to continue, feeling nauseous. "What you did for me—well, it was more than I ever expected. I just wanted to make sure you know how much I appreciate it."

"What are friends for, if not to chase away stalkers?" Nick joked. When she didn't smile, his eyes narrowed. "You haven't heard from him, have you?"

"No. Why?" Panic reached out and clamped its hand around her throat, taking away her breath. Her fingers involuntarily pinched the fabric of her capris. "Have you heard something?"

"Me?" Nick shook his head, his face confused as he studied her. "No."

"Oh. Good." She knew she'd just made a fool of herself with her reaction, but she still struggled with a sense of dread. "I—I never heard from him again after you read him the riot act."

"That's great." Nick kept looking at her. "Isn't it?"

Shay offered an unconvincing nod, still unable to shake her memories of those horrible days.

When the police couldn't help, she'd fought to hold her world together on her own. And she'd been losing that war, until Nick arrived. She'd been so relieved to see a friend that day that she'd dumped the whole sorry tale on his broad shoulders. Being the good guy he was, Nick had insisted on knowing the details. Then he'd heard Dom's voice, demeaning, threatening and mocking her.

Shay couldn't believe it when Nick told Dom he'd taped the conversation and threatened police action and reprisals from what Nick claimed were legions of Shay's friends. It worked—she'd never heard from the stalker again—but she'd never been able to shed the panic from those months of persecution. She always felt Dom was out there, lurking, waiting for her weakest moment to appear again.

"Did you ever figure out why this guy focused on you?"

"No. The first couple of times he emailed me through my fan page, he was very nice. He complimented me on my latest cover, said he'd seen me on a talk show, asked if I might throw my support behind a pet hospital, that kind of thing. He was very friendly." Shivers speed-walked up her spine. "But by the time you came to New York, he'd become very aggressive. He told me he'd touched me without my realizing it. I didn't believe him, but then he gave details and I knew he'd been near. Too near."

"Nobody ever remembered seeing him?"

"No, and believe me, I questioned everyone, though I never actually told anyone what was going on. Later I learned some of the other models had faced the same thing, so they would have understood how worried I was, but..." She shrugged. "At the time I was too scared and embarrassed to talk about it."

"Maybe he was someone you worked with." Nick's lips tightened into a grim line.

"I thought of that. But I never had any concrete proof to give police, no personal details. After the fourth or fifth call, I think they stopped believing me. And he knew it."

"Hey, relax now. You're safe here," Nick reminded her.

"Yes." Shay inhaled to regain control. "It's just...I have no idea how he found my number or knew my new address. I changed phones and moved, but that only seemed to aggravate him. Police traced the calls, but they always led to a dead end. Dom was very careful. When he did call—well, you heard him. He'd taunt me with what he'd do when we were alone—" She gulped and forced her breathing to slow. "Sorry. I still struggle a bit with his—you know."

"Abuse." Nick's cold, hard word made her flinch.

"Well, yes." She exhaled. "I tried a hundred different things. I ignored him. I monitored every move I made to see if I could figure out who he was. I became suspicious of everyone. But I was helpless. I had no idea how to—" Shay paused. It sounded weak and pathetic to say escape, as if she'd been a prisoner. Yet that was exactly what she'd felt like.

"Shay, that kind of guy preys on people through fear. But he's gone. You can forget about him now." He studied her.

"I know. I will be fine," Shay said, determined to make it so.

When she thought about how it all began, she felt foolish. Too well she recalled how the innocent-seeming online friendship had changed into something menacing after Dom had found out she'd given the flowers he sent her to someone else. That's when she'd started to feel uncomfortable. But she didn't think of contacting the police until odd messages were left on her voice mail. Crazy, untraceable phone calls showed up on her cell when she went to lunch with her friends or took a break at work. He always seemed to know where she was. But worst of all were his increasingly hateful comments. They seemed to hint that violence could explode if she said or did something to provoke him, and that had scared her into a shivering mass of fear.

Until Nick, her rescuer, arrived.

But even after, even when she'd left New York and modeling, it had taken months of intense therapy to attain an occasional night of uninterrupted sleep, free of his voice, his taunts that he would find her when she least expected it. Those words haunted her, so much so that they'd ruined her relationship with Eric, the man she thought she loved. She could barely breathe when his arms closed around her—all she wanted was to run from him. Finally her memories had pushed Eric away and she'd lost what she wanted most—love.

Still Shay was determined she would vanquish Dom and overcome the terror that he'd planted in her brain.

Please, God?

Nick must have read the tumult of emotions in her eyes. He leaned forward, his dark eyes almost hidden beneath his jutting brow, and spoke slowly but with unshakeable resolve.

"Shay, you cannot spend the rest of your life worrying about whether or not this crazy person will come back."

"I know." She inhaled. "I'm here in Hope to start over. And I'm really trying. It's just—I can't seem to forget the ugly things he said."

"You will."

"Can you imagine if anyone besides you had overheard his words to me?" Her cheeks burned. "I would have felt so ashamed. The things he said—" She couldn't go there. Not with Nick watching her. "I'm ashamed that I couldn't stop him on my own."

"You did the best you could, Shay."

"Did I?" She shook her head. "I wonder about that now."

"Why do you doubt yourself?" Nick demanded.

"It would have been better if I'd told more people about him." Keeping her secret had weighed heavily. Even Eric hadn't known until that last, horrible date, and by then he didn't want any explanations—he wanted a girlfriend who showed her love, not some shrinking violet afraid to let him even kiss her cheek. But tonight, with her friend Nick, it felt good to talk about what she'd kept hidden for so long. "But I was worried that stories would leak out. I had sponsors and a lot of media attention then."

"I remember you came out in support of that kids' charity around that time, too," Nick said. His brown eyes gleamed. "Just getting to share a cup of coffee with you made me feel like I'd won a triathlon."

"Silly." She smiled at him but felt compelled to keep explaining. "My agent was afraid that if I went public, it might have brought more weirdos out of the woodwork."

"Too bad he didn't try to stop the jerk." Nick's grim face expressed his opinion.

"My agent was a she," Shay protested mildly, warmed by his caring. "And she's the one who first insisted I call the police. That didn't help, so I did the only thing I could think to do and pretended everything was all right." She made a face. "But eventually I couldn't pretend well enough. I knew Dad had always wanted me to reach the top but he was gone and I was scared and lonely so I decided it was time to move on, to fulfill my promise to join Jessica's clinic. And now here I am." She was not going to tell Nick about her crippling panic attacks—he didn't need to know everything.

"I'm glad you're here." His brown eyes crinkled at the corners as he smiled.

"Thanks." Her heart gave a bump at his kindness. "Anyway, that brings me to the reason I asked you to come tonight."

"Maggie. Yeah, I wanted to talk to you about her, too. You go first."

"Okay. Well, I met with her doctors this morning. They asked me to start on her therapy immediately." Shay wasn't sure how well Nick understood what Maggie's future would entail so she proceeded cautiously. "Has anyone said anything to you about her progress?"

"The doctor today said Maggie isn't doing as well as he'd hoped, but I don't know exactly what that means."

"Maggie's internal injuries have healed very well, according to the reports," Shay began. "Though her leg muscles were badly damaged when she was crushed inside the car, the surgery appears to have been successful. Yet Maggie hasn't regained her strength." Shay studied his face. "You must have noticed that."

"She can't bear her own weight yet, if that's what you mean."

"She should be able to do that by now, Nick. In fact, Maggie should be walking." Shay reached out and touched his fingers, hoping that would ease what she was about to say. But she had to draw back or risk exposing her anxiety. "The fact that she can't even stand is a bad sign. It means she's losing her mobility much faster than anyone thought."

"My medical knowledge wouldn't fill a teaspoon, Shay. Talk to me plainly and bluntly," he demanded.

"Unless Maggie regains her mobility soon, there's a strong possibility she will never walk normally again." Shay watched horror fill his face.

"But she does exercises," Nick protested.

"Your mom does them with her?" Shay waited for his nod. "All the time?"

Nick's face altered.

"I'm guessing she skips them sometimes because Maggie says they hurt too much." From the look on his face Shay knew she was right. "Your mom probably hasn't felt able to make the long, twice-weekly drives to Las Cruces for therapy either."

"No. But they're just little leg lifts and things. It's no big deal," Nick argued.

"You're an athlete, Nick. You know how quickly the body loses muscle strength if it's not regularly used." Shay tried to make him understand. "You probably still follow a post-surgical therapy program to keep your shoulder from tightening up. Right?"

"Yes." He flexed his arm as if she'd reminded him.

"It's the same for Maggie. In the months she was in traction and healing from her internal injuries, there was little to be done except let her heal. Now she's done that."

"The doctor said that today," he admitted.

"She should be moving by now. Yet on the swing today, you saw that she could barely point her toes. That's not good." Shay wasn't finished, but Nick's sudden shifting in his chair made her wonder if he'd hear all she had to say?

"I don't mean to, but I think I hurt her when I lift her," Nick confessed, his guilt-filled stare lifting to meet her gaze.

Shay nodded. "But that's primarily because she has no strength to lift herself and ease the strain. She's barely using her leg muscles at all from what I saw." This was the hardest part, getting people to see what was only visible to the trained eye. "Maggie's become too comfortable with being carried. She makes no demands of her body. My hunch is that no one's challenged her to do more."

Nick sat still, assimilating her words. Then he looked up.

Sun-streaked wisps of hair had drifted onto his broad forehead, and in that moment he looked very much like the determined teenage boy who'd once proclaimed he would never be anything like the father who had abandoned him.

"I refuse to accept that my sister's child will never walk again if it's even remotely possible that she can," he said, his voice tight with control. "So what do we do?"

"We get Maggie moving, Nick," Shay said with a grin, delighted by his response. "It won't be easy and it won't be fun, but it will work if we don't give up. Are you up for it?"

"Me?" He gaped at her, eyes wide with surprise. "But my mother—"

"Your mother can't do this, Nick. She's too close to Maggie and in too much pain herself. I saw her at the grocery store. Her hands must be killing her."

"Uh—" Nick gulped as Shay held his gaze and laid out the blunt truth.

"If you commit to overseeing Maggie's treatment, this will be totally on you. Are you sure you have what it takes to get it done?"

"Of course I do," he growled, lips drawn tight.

"You won't be Maggie's favorite uncle anymore, Nick. In fact, she might even hate you for putting her through the pain."

Nick's eyes darkened to almost black. "You're saying...?"

"Maybe you should think about finding someone else to do this?" Shay asked, hoping that he wouldn't.

"Like who?" he demanded. "My sisters? Cara's got her hands full with twins. Lara travels constantly for her job. And let's just say Simone has enough trouble that I have no intention of adding to it. There is nobody else, Shay." Nick studied her, old friend to old friend. "To clarify, you're saying that if Maggie follows a regimen you cook up, she will be able to walk?"

"I'm ninety percent sure she could regain all of her mobility."

"Ninety percent?" Nick frowned. "Not completely sure then?"

"No." Shay had to tell him the total truth. "But I am one hundred percent sure that if things continue as they have been, your niece will be confined to a wheelchair in one year. Maybe less."

Nick fell back into his chair as if he'd been slapped. "Are you serious?"

"Very." Shay nodded. The bald truth. He deserved it. So did Maggie. "Left unused, within the year the ligaments will lose their pliability, her leg muscles will degenerate, and then there will no longer be an opportunity for Maggie to regain her mobility."

Nick spent several long moments in silent contemplation. When he finally lifted his head, Shay's heart ached for the sadness clouding his beautiful eyes. He cleared his throat, then spoke, his voice ragged.

"How long will it take?"

"I don't know. Four months, maybe six. Maybe longer." She shrugged. "After I do more tests, I'll have a better idea, but the end result is going to depend on whether or not we can get Maggie motivated."

"I see." He nodded, his head drooped low.

"Think long and hard before you commit to this, Nick," Shay told him. "Maggie needs someone who will be there day after day, holding her accountable. She must have a coach who won't give up, no matter what, and is committed for as long as it takes."

He lifted his head. His eyes, deep-set beneath his broad, tanned forehead, silently begged her to understand his quandary.

"I only have six months here in Hope. Then I start my new job in Seattle. I can't stay longer than that, Shay. I mean, I want to but—" He clamped his lips together.

Shay said nothing, allowing him the space to deal with all he'd just learned.

"I can't just leave Maggie the way she is, knowing she'll never walk again." Nick's tortured tone stabbed her aching heart. "Her mom would hate that. You know how active Georgia was."

Shay did know. Nick's sister Georgia had been her coach when she'd decided to run a marathon in her senior year. No one could have pushed her harder than Georgia.

"But Georgia isn't here anymore, Nick," she said quietly. "You are. You and I."

She hated that she'd added more to his already topsy-turvy world. It had only been a short time ago that Nick had found out his career was over. Then he'd lost his sister and his niece had been orphaned. His whole world was in flux.

"If it's impossible for you, you might be able to hire a personal trainer or someone else to be Maggie's helper," she added, offering him a way out.

"Nobody with those qualifications stays in a little place like Hope," he said, his voice edged with frustration. "So they'd leave and we'd be back in the same situation. Maggie would suffer." He shook his head. "Any other ideas?"

"No. I'm sorry. All I can tell you is that I don't want to wait on this. I want to get Maggie started on a strengthening routine as soon as possible. Tomorrow would be good." Shay held her breath, waiting for his response.

After a long pause he asked, "What time tomorrow?"

"Eight in the morning. Till noon."

"I see." He rose wearily. "I've got to think about this. About what it will mean," he added. "And I have to discuss it with Mom. She'll make the final decision."

"Of course." Shay stood, too. As she looked up at Nick, she realized that she'd always liked that he stood six feet two inches, just three inches taller than her, tall enough that at the prom she'd been able to lay her head on his shoulder. She wished she could do that now.

"I never finished my college degree, you know. I don't have anything else to fall back on but this job the team offered." Nick's eyes grew muddy with confusion. "Even so, my first priority is always to my family."

"Of course." Anyone who knew Nick knew that about him. "Maybe the team would grant you an extension?"

"They already have—that's why I'm here. But if I'm not back on the appointed day, I have no job." He shook his head. "It probably sounds pretentious, but I have to capitalize on my fame as the winningest quarterback in history while it's still fresh in everyone's mind. I'm only good for endorsements till the next star comes along. If I let this job go—" He left it hanging. After a moment Nick regrouped and straightened his shoulders. "I'll have Maggie at the clinic tomorrow morning at eight. And I'll have a decision for you then, too."

"Great." Shay stood on her porch, watching as Nick walked slowly to his truck. He opened the door then stopped.

"Shay?"

"Yes?" Her heart ached for the once-fun-loving guy who'd been her white knight. She wanted to tell him it didn't matter, but it did.

"Thank you." His dark eyes met hers. "Telling me all this can't have been easy for you."

"No," she said quietly. "The truth is often very painful. But don't worry, Nick—I make sure my kids get the very best."

"Your kids." A smile drifted across his face then flickered away as he stared directly into her eyes. "And you think I'm 'the best' for Maggie?"

"Yes." she nodded. "I do. You and your mom care about her more than any hired person ever could."

"Yeah, we do. Okay, then. Good night."

"Good night, Nick."

Shay remained standing on her porch until Nick and his truck disappeared from sight. Then she holed up in her study and worked most of the night refining her rehabilitation plan for Maggie. Nick would do it, she was almost positive of that. He was that kind of man. Family mattered to him more than anything else in the world. But what she wasn't so sure of was if he would leave when his six months were up or if he'd continue for as long as Maggie needed him.

A yearning for a family like his—for the knowledge that someone would be there for you, to share the good times and bad—ached inside Shay and would not be soothed no matter how many of her blessings she recounted.

Her parents were gone. Brianna and Jaclyn had their own lives. Of course Shay was delighted that both of them had found love, but it meant that the tight bond between the three of them had changed. It also meant she was the only one with no one of her own.

Shay had tried so hard to trust Eric when he said he would wait for her to get over her panic attacks. But she'd jerked away one too many times and he had eventually given up on her. He'd left her.

Everyone left.

That's why she had to get these anxiety issues under control.

Because though Shay intended to spend the rest of her life alone, she was not going to spend it mourning the past. She was going to help kids. Especially Maggie.

Nick would help Maggie as much as he could, too, but after six months, she was fairly certain, he would leave Hope and resume his football career. It was up to Shay to get Maggie as mobile as possible before he went. She'd deal with her problems privately, with God's help.

"Thank You for this new home and this new life, Lord," she whispered as the first peach fingers of dawn crept over the jagged tips of the Organ Mountains.

She'd been given so much. Now it was time to give back.

Surely, helping Maggie and the rest of Hope's kids would satisfy the longing of her heart.

Chapter Three

Nick sat on his mother's deck with Shay's words running through his mind as warm spring rain pattered down on the awning above him.

Staying in Hope for who knew how long—at least until Maggie was walking—would cost him his future.

Why? he asked God. *You took my career. Okay, so I'll start over. But I only have six months here. Then I have to go.*

It wasn't that Nick didn't love Maggie. He wanted to see Georgia's daughter walk again with every fiber of his being.

But if he took on her therapy and it took longer than six months, what would he do about his future?

Confusion filled him. He'd been so certain the coaching job in Seattle was God's answer to his prayer. Helping his mom with Maggie was supposed to give him time to prepare for the only job he felt qualified for.

But if I'm not supposed to do that job, what am *I supposed to do, God?*

When no miraculous way out presented itself, Nick considered his options.

He could take Maggie with him, back to Seattle.

He discarded that immediately. Even if he did hire someone to work with Maggie, his mom wouldn't want to move back there. And Nick was pretty sure his mom would never allow her grandchild to live so far away from her.

Maybe he could hire someone in town, as Shay had suggested.

Nick scratched that idea, too. He'd already phoned around. Hope didn't have someone of the caliber he needed for Maggie. And if he hired a certified trainer to come to Hope, he'd be too far away to keep an eye on things. Plus, if he spent his savings on Maggie, what would he do if his mom or sisters needed money? His savings would be gone and his dad sure couldn't be counted on to help.

Defeat swamped Nick as he finally accepted that he had no choice. He would stay in Hope for however long it took to help Maggie. He'd stay and play the heavy and push her even when she cried for mercy.

He dreaded that most of all.

Nick had been through therapy. He remembered too well the days it took every effort just to show up. But he'd done it because, in the back of his mind, he'd hoped he could get back in the game, get his life back. Maggie wouldn't have that drive. She was just a little kid. The intense therapy Shay was talking about would hurt her. But if, as Shay said, the only alternative was a wheelchair, he could not—would not—back down. She had to do it.

"What are you doing out here, son?" His mother handed him a steaming mug.

Nick took it and smiled. Peppermint tea, her panacea for all of life's ills.

"You do know it's past two-thirty?"

"I know. Just thinking." He couldn't tell her what was on his heart. His mother would feel responsible. If she guessed his fears, she might insist on moving back to Seattle for his sake, and he knew how little she wanted to leave her friends, her home and the desert dryness that eased her arthritic pain.

"Shay's plan—it's going to be hard on Maggie, Mom. Really hard."

"I know. I should have pushed the child to do more, but—"

"No." He wouldn't let her feel guilty. "What you did was good. But now it's going to get intense. Shay says Maggie has to get walking, and soon."

"I've been praying about that." His mother sat down next to him on the built-in bench that ran the length of the deck, a small part of the extensive renovations he'd had done on her house after he'd signed his first big contract. "I know God has a plan in all this, but I just can't see it," she said, sniffling.

"Me neither," Nick muttered, trying to suppress his frustration. As his mother's tears spilled down her cheeks, he lifted his arm and hugged her against his shoulder. "Don't cry, Mom. We have to be strong now. For Maggie."

"You've always been a pillar of strength to me, son. I thank God for you every day." Before Nick could say anything further, she'd launched into a prayer that included him, Maggie, Shay and half the town of Hope. That was Mom, always talking to God about every detail in her world.

Nick only half listened. Lately his communication with heaven seemed distinctly one-sided. Probably had something to do with what he felt was the unfairness of his world. First his career, then his sister. Now it seemed God wanted his job, too.

When his mom finished praying, she lifted her head to smile at him.

"I'm going to bed. You should go, too. You'll need your rest to help Maggie." She rose, held out a hand.

"Don't worry about me. I'm fine." Nick took her hand, gently squeezed the gnarled fingers and brushed a kiss against her silvery head. "I'll be up shortly, Mom. You go ahead."

"Don't fret, Nick. God will handle everything. After all, He sent us Shay. Aren't you glad she's back?"

"Yeah." And he was, Nick realized. He didn't know anyone else he'd rather work with on Maggie's care.

"You two always made such a great pair. You always seem so perfectly matched, as if you can read each other's minds." She smiled. "You were always inseparable."

"Maybe when we were kids." But Nick heard a note in her voice that made him study her face. "There's nothing between Shay and I now, Mom. We're just friends."

"But good friends, right? And who knows when that could change."

Oh, yeah, she was implying something more than friendship all right.

"It's not going to change, Mom. It can't. Shay knows that in six months I'm leaving town. And she's staying here, at the clinic. But in the meantime we're both going to do the best we can for Mags."

"I know you will," his mom said soberly. "You'll be perfect together."

"I don't know about that." He grimaced. "We'll probably argue. As Shay reminded me, therapy isn't fun. I don't mind for myself, but I wish I could make things easier for Maggie."

"You and Shay will find a way to help her," his mother assured him. "Put you two together and the world of possibilities is huge. I just need to have faith that God is going to use both of you to do wonderful things for my granddaughter." She kissed him on his forehead the same way she did with Maggie, took his empty mug and walked inside.

Nick waited until the light in her room blinked out, doubting she'd heard his warning that nothing more than friendship was going to happen between him and Shay. Knowing there was no way he could sleep with everything whirling around in his head, Nick walked over to the old shed he'd taken refuge in when he was eleven, the day his dad had left them. It wasn't much back then, but it was where he'd first begun tinkering with his mom's vacuum and later found out he had a knack for adapting machines. The old shed had been revamped and modified as his inventing took over. When he'd had his mom's house renovated, Nick had more electrical outlets added and installed more tools and a better workbench to the shed.

Christmas, holidays, celebrations—he came out here every time he came home, relishing the fact that no matter how long he was away or how far removed Hope seemed from the rest of his world, the peaceful ambience in the shed never changed. Coming in here gave him the same satisfaction it had as a kid—here, he could let his imagination take flight. He flicked on the light and studied the assortment of his inventions that he'd unearthed the past few days.

His mom had said God sent them Shay. He had to agree. The fact that Shay was going to help Maggie walk again filled him with a feeling he couldn't quite describe. It was deep gratitude, of course, but it was also something else, something that made him a little uneasy. All he knew was that he had to bring his A game to this whole process—he didn't want to let anybody down. Least of all Shay.

Nick reached down and picked up a gizmo he'd invented years ago. It gave him an idea. If he could come up with something fun, something that kept his niece's attention off her pain and encouraged her to take another step, that would push her to work harder and help both Shay and him be more effective. And it would also help him keep his mind off whatever it was he was feeling about Shay Parker.

"Uncle Nick? Where are you, Uncle Nick?"

Nick jerked awake, suddenly aware that the desert sun shone through the small shed windows with a strength that said he was very late.

"Uncle Nick!"

"I'm coming." Nick shut off the lights and laid a tarp over his work. Fiddling with it felt good but it was probably a waste of time because, despite the hours he'd spent scouring the internet for information on Maggie's injury, he still wasn't sure of exactly what he was trying to accomplish. He turned his back on the mess he'd created and walked into the yard.

"Hey, pumpkin."

"Did you go to bed last night?" Maggie's brown eyes stretched wide.

"Nope. Working." He let one of her ringlets twine itself around his finger.

"Can I see?" Maggie asked eagerly. She was sitting on the porch swing he'd had installed last Mother's Day. From the corner of his eye, Nick saw Maggie move. With the tiniest movement of her body Maggie had managed to put the swing into motion. It was the first time he'd seen her extend such an effort. Excitement filled him, but he kept his cool.

"Uncle Nick, did you get something working?" Maggie pressed.

"Not yet. It won't do what I want."

"It will. You can build anything. Remember that robot you made at Christmas? I love your inventions." Maggie's smile had a child's blithe confidence of a world where good always triumphed. If she could see the good in things, Nick felt challenged to rid himself of his feelings of defeat

"Grandma says you're taking me to see Shay today."

"What do you think of that?" he asked, watching her face.

Maggie shrugged. "Is she a doctor like Aunty Jaclyn?"

"No. She works at the same clinic, but Shay's a physiotherapist. She helps people use their muscles," Nick explained.

"Grandma says she's going to help me walk again." Maggie's voice trembled slightly.

"Would you like that?" He held his breath waiting for her response.

"Yes!" Her eyes glittered with excitement. "Staying with Grandma is nice, but I want to go to school like other kids do."

"It's going to take a lot of hard work, Mags, and it might hurt," he warned.

"It hurts now," Maggie said, fear in her eyes.

"Once your muscles get used to working, I don't think it will hurt so much anymore. We can ask Shay about that. Okay?" Nick waited for her nod, satisfied that at least she was willing to try, even if she didn't yet know what was to come. "Well, I'd better shower and get changed. Are you okay here for now?"

Maggie nodded. Then, with the slightest stretch she again touched her toe against the floor and pushed. A hiss of pain escaped her lips, but as the swing moved she grinned. "I prayed and asked God to help me to walk again.

"Good for you." Nick stemmed the urge to tell her not to try too hard. Because according to Shay, that was exactly what Maggie would have to do in the coming months.

She seemed up for it. But was he?

You have to be. This is no different from when Dad walked out and left Mom with five kids to feed.

As the eldest, Nick had taken very seriously the responsibility of making sure his family was okay. Just as he had back then, he would now put aside his own plans for the good of the family.

He'd ignored his counselor's advice to get his engineering degree because football was in his heart and a career with the pigskin was the quickest way to give his family all the things his father hadn't. And he'd never regretted that choice. But now that playing football was over, Nick felt he'd lost the one thing that had provided him with a sense of security and made him feel competent in his caregiver role. He needed the coaching job so he'd be able to confront his father in his mind and say, "See, even though I'm out of the game, I'm still not like you. I'm not walking away from my family."

Like his father cared. He'd written them all out of his life.

"I need that job, God," Nick whispered, self-conscious about his prayer. "But I want Maggie walking more. Can You make both of them happen?"

As prayers went, it wasn't stellar. And Nick didn't hear a heavenly response inside or outside his head. He'd have to check in with God again later. Right now it was time to take Maggie to Shay's office for her first therapy session.

"Maggie, do you want to walk again?"

Shay crouched in front of the little girl, blocking her view of Nick watching from the sidelines.

"Yes."

"Do you want it enough to keep trying when Uncle Nick asks you to, even though it hurts?" She saw fear creep into Maggie's big round eyes and laid a reassuring hand on the child's thin arm.

"I—I think so," came the whispered response.

Shay lifted one eyebrow.

"I want to walk." Maggie's chin jutted out. "I am going to walk."

"Atta girl." Shay hugged her, loving the spirit she saw in the child's brown eyes. "Now that we've stretched, let's see how your legs feel about walking." She ignored Nick's gasp and eased Maggie into a standing position. She carefully guided one foot forward, ensuring Maggie had a hold of the rails on each side of her.

"Ow!" Maggie cried out.

Shay sensed more than saw Nick jerk upright.

"I know it hurts, honey. Your legs are mad. You haven't used them for a long time and they've gotten lazy. They like having Uncle Nick and Grandma carry you around." Shay kept working as she spoke. "You lazy legs! You've been on a long holiday, but your vacation is over now. It's time for you to get to work."

A couple of minutes were all Maggie could bear upright, but that was okay. They'd taken the first step, literally. Shay helped her lie down on a floor mat then massaged her muscles until they were relaxed.

"See over there, Maggie?" She pointed to the corner of the room. "There's a video camera there. It took pictures of you when you walked today. Each time you come here we're going to take more pictures. Then, in a little while, you'll be able to see how the exercises are helping. Are you ready to do more now?"

Maggie frowned. "I guess so."

"Good." Shay motioned Nick over so he could watch and repeat each stretching move she made. When Maggie winced and attempted to pull away, Shay reassured her, keeping her distracted with a silly game for each exercise. When Nick didn't use enough force, Shay laid her hands on top of his and guided his movements. The contact gave her a nervous quiver in the pit of her stomach. She wished his touch didn't make her want to jerk away from him.

When would she be able to move on from those memories?

"Good job," Shay praised after an hour had passed. She grinned at Nick. "And you, too."

"Are we finished now?" Maggie's red face shone with perspiration. "'Cause I'm tired."

"It is time for a break. You worked very hard, honey. I'm so proud of you." Shay hugged the little girl.

"Uncle Nick worked hard, too," Maggie said. "Aren't you going to hug him?"

"I think Uncle Nick's too big for hugs," Shay said, nonplussed by the child's comment.

"Nobody's ever too big for a hug. That's what Grandma says." Maggie waited.

Uncomfortable, already way too aware of Nick, Shay had little choice but to place her arms around his waist and hug him. She pulled away quickly as panic knotted her insides.

"Shortest hug in history," Nick complained. His teasing grin made her blush.

Shay swallowed hard and admitted the hard truth to herself. It wasn't just panic that had her pulling away from Nick so quickly. It was something else, something that made her wonder what it would be like to really hug him, not as the friend she remembered from high school, but as the devastatingly handsome man he'd become, a man who made her wish he'd hug her back.

That made her really nervous.

"Now, Maggie," Shay said, hurrying to get her focus back on task. "I want you to rest—I'll give you a juice box and a book. Then, after you have rested, there are a few other things we need to go through."

"I can't really read yet," Maggie mumbled, her cheeks reddening.

"Oh, you'll be able to read this." Shay handed her a book specially designed for preschool kids. Soon the room was filled with the recorded sounds of barnyard animals telling a story. "We'll be back in a minute. You stay there, okay, honey?"

Maggie nodded absently, already enthralled by the story. Shay motioned to Nick to follow her outside. She led the way to her office, made them each a cup of coffee and then sat down.

"So that's the first part. What do you think?" Shay deliberately chose the chair behind her desk instead of sitting next to him, where she usually sat with most caregivers. But then again, most caregivers didn't have the strange effect on her that Nick Green seemed to be having today. Just thinking about that hug made her take a minute to control her rapid breathing. "Okay?" she asked.

"I think I can manage. As long as I don't hurt her."

"She'll tell you if you do. Go slowly. Warm up thoroughly at first with the stretches." She leaned forward, intent on making him understand. "Don't skip anything, Nick. Each move is designed to prepare for the one that follows." She checked the closed-circuit monitor on her desk to ensure Maggie was still resting and reading. "She's a great little girl. I think she'll do well."

"As long as I don't mess up," Nick muttered as he stared at his hands. His troubled gaze met hers. "She's so—delicate."

A rush of heat warmed Shay's heart. Nick was always concerned about his precious family. One glance at her appointment book told her she shouldn't make the offer she was about to make, but Nick had been there for her when she'd needed him most. She had to help him now.

"I could come to your mom's place tomorrow morning to watch you go through your paces the first time. If you'd like," she offered.

"Would you?" Relief flooded his handsome face. "I'd really appreciate it. That way Mom could watch, too, just in case I have to be away or something."

Shay's heart sank at the words, but she struggled to sound detached.

"Nick, I told you last night. This can't be hit or miss. Maggie needs the same routine every day. Besides, I doubt your mom could manage all the manipulations Maggie needs. You have to do it, no matter how unpleasant."

"You're making it sound like I'm trying to get out of helping Maggie." His face tightened with irritation.

"Are you?" she asked, keeping her voice even.

Anger lit a fire in his dark eyes. "I'm here, okay, Shay? I

will be here for however long it takes. In the event something comes up, we'll work it out together. Okay?" When she nodded he put his cup down and rose to his full height. "Let's get on with it," he said in a flat voice.

Nick walked out of the room. Knowing he was frustrated with her, Shay kept her distance until they reached her treatment room.

"I'm sorry if I irritated you, Nick. But Maggie has to be my first concern. You understand that, don't you?"

"Yes." He sighed. "Forget it, okay?"

"Okay," she agreed. She laid her hand on the doorknob then froze when his covered hers a millisecond later. In a flash, panic swamped her and she flinched away from his touch.

"Shay?" When she didn't answer, Nick tipped her chin up so she had to look at him. She tried not to flinch again. "What's wrong?"

Stupid. Stupid. Stupid. She tried to avert her eyes but couldn't. "N-nothing. I'm fine."

"That's not true." His brows drew together as their gazes locked. "You're shaking," he said in surprise.

"I'm fine, Nick."

"Sure you are. That's why you're acting like I'm going to hurt you." His eyes blazed. She could almost hear his perfect, even teeth grit together. "I am not your stalker, Shay."

"I know that." She tried to move away to gather her composure, but he blocked her path.

Nick's face softened. "He sure did a number on you. Did you ever get some help?"

"I'm fine." Shay laid her hand on the knob again, eager to get his attention off her.

"You're not fine." Nick reached out as if to touch her cheek, saw the way she recoiled from him and let his hand fall to his side. "Obviously," he murmured.

"I will be."

"Oh, Shay. You can't make yourself be fine any more than Maggie can." He lowered his voice. "Promise me you'll talk to Brianna."

"The thing is, I have to handle this myself, Nick, in my own way. And I will." Embarrassed, she dragged open the door and pasted on her brightest smile. "Okay, Maggie. How was the book? Are you ready for some more work?"

Behind her Nick said nothing. But throughout the entire session she could feel his intense scrutiny. Shay knew she had to get a better grip on her reactions or risk Nick seeing just how out of control her panic attacks had become.

Coming home, back to Hope, was Shay's fresh start. She would not allow the past to tarnish her life here. A nice guy like Nick—her friend—didn't deserve the way she shrunk away from him.

Tonight she'd study her self-help book some more, see if she could discover a new technique to suppress her fear. She'd pray longer, harder. Somehow she would figure out a way to be whole again, to heal that scar her stalker had left her with.

She knew there was nothing to fear in Hope. Nothing at all.

So why was she still terrified?

Chapter Four

"A little more pressure right here, Nick. More. Good."

Two mornings later Nick steeled himself against Maggie's whimper of pain while Shay's hands guided his. She'd had to cancel yesterday but had shown up bright and smiling right after breakfast this morning. As she bent to smile encouragement at him, her shimmering hair brushed his cheek. He caught his breath at the soft floral fragrance and immediately recalled that day in New York when he'd helped her untangle her hair from her sunglasses. Despite everything that had happened, Shay Parker was still the most beautiful woman he knew. His heart-thudding reaction to her was perfectly normal. Any red-blooded male would respond to Shay's smile.

They'd been at it for an hour and Nick was more tired than he'd ever been, including after his first championship game. Would he ever get used to the feeling that he was torturing Maggie?

"Sweetie, that was fantastic." Shay apparently had no issues with hugging his niece, though she still edged away from Nick whenever he got too close. He despised her stalker for that legacy.

"Grandma and I prayed God would help me." Maggie

swiped at a tear that lingered on her cheek. "It didn't hurt *too* much."

"I promise it will hurt less each time and pretty soon it won't hurt at all. Okay?" Shay squeezed Maggie's shoulder. "Just don't give up."

"I won't." The child thrust out her chin. "I want to walk by my own self."

Nick heaved a sigh of relief. Maybe he hadn't done so badly today.

"When can I ride Uncle Nick's roly-poly?"

"His what?" Shay looked from Maggie to him, then back to Maggie, one perfect eyebrow arched. "What's a roly-poly?"

"It's an invention Uncle Nick made. And it's way cool." Maggie's eyes danced as she struggled to sit up. "It's kind of like—it makes noises and—you tell her, Uncle Nick."

"It's just a gizmo I've been fooling around with. Roly-poly is Maggie's name for it." Once he'd figured out exactly which muscles Shay was targeting, Nick had spent most of yesterday tweaking his prototype.

He was *not* ready for anyone to see it, but he should have expected Maggie to tell Shay about it. She was enthralled with the bells, whistles and whirly gigs he'd attached so that every movement made a noise.

"Can I see it?" Shay must have remembered his reluctance in high school to show off his devices before he'd completed them because she paused a moment, then softly added, "Please?"

He guessed she wanted to see if what he was making would cause Maggie problems.

"Sure." Nick rose from the floor, helped Maggie into her chair and pushed it up to the table, where his mother waited with a drawing tablet and art pencils. "I'll be back in a few minutes, Mom."

"No rush," she said with a smile. She was always smiling,

in spite of the pain he knew plagued her joints. Nick remembered asking her once why she was always so happy. "Because God loves me," she'd told him. He'd never quite grasped the comfort she found in that, though he'd often wished he could. Once, in high school, after he'd told Shay he struggled to feel God's love ever since his dad had dumped them, Shay had admitted she felt the same way after her mom died. He wondered if she still felt like that.

"You've been working in the shed again," Shay exclaimed as she followed him outside. "Remember the time you were trying to figure out a sequence for the Fourth of July fireworks? You almost blew off the roof." She laughed, her eyes crinkling at the corners.

"Go ahead, make fun of me," he growled and blocked the door. As he looked down at her, he realized he wasn't that much taller than Shay, but somehow she always brought out a protective urge in him. Maybe it was the innocence in her wide-open gaze or the way she always looked directly at him, as if she expected nothing but the truth from him. His heart seemed to skip a beat at the thought, and he cleared his throat. "Maybe I shouldn't let you see what I've been working on."

"I'm just teasing." Her smile softened. "I also remember how you constructed that ladder thing that let Mrs. Smith get what she needed from her attic without endangering herself. And the way you rigged that gizmo in Mr. Murphy's garage so he could raise and lower shelves. And—"

"Okay. Enough ego boosting," he said in his drollest tone.

"Your inventions have made a difference to quite a few people in Hope, Nick."

"For that you are permitted to enter, kind madam." He bowed and waved a hand as if granting passage into a secret cave. Well, it *was* his man cave.

Shay walked inside and stopped, her head swiveling to

take in the assortment of projects on his workbench. "It's not exactly the same as it used to be."

"I should hope not. I'm older and smarter now." He grinned when she rolled her eyes. He directed her to his left. "This is what Maggie was talking about," he said, pointing to the roly-poly.

Shay bent to study his work. "Interesting. What is it, exactly?"

"I researched Maggie's injury. Then, after watching you work with her, I put this together. It's like a walker. Sort of." Unnerved by Shay's silence, Nick lifted it and set it in front of her. "When you push it, it makes noise. I figured it might keep her from getting bored with the exercises."

"Clever guy," Shay murmured. She pushed the handle and grinned at the noise that followed.

"Once she's mastered this, it won't take much to change it up a bit," Nick explained. "Maybe I'll make it more like a bicycle that she has to pedal. That would build strength in her legs, wouldn't it?"

"Yes, it would." Shay asked him to demonstrate so she could watch which muscles he used—Nick began to sweat bullets wondering if he'd made a huge mistake. Then Shay tried it herself. "It's amazing," she said. "Ingenious, actually. Obviously Maggie can hardly wait to try it, and those things that whirl and click and beep will be an excellent incentive for her to push harder to make them go faster, louder, whatever."

"I hope so." He adjusted one of the handlebars trying to hide his delight that Shay thought his work was amazing. "It needs a few modifications but it'll soon be finished. When do you think she could start using it?"

"Whenever she wants to give it a shot." Shay straightened. "But only where it's flat and smooth. And only if you're right beside her. She will tire quickly at first and may overbalance. Don't let her overdo."

"I could add something like training wheels," he mused. "That would provide stability."

"Good idea." She moved to study another machine he was deconstructing. "What's this?"

"It was going to be an adaptation to the pedal system on Mom's old bike, to make riding easier. She promised Maggie they'd take a bike ride when she's able," Nick explained. "But I can't get it to work right so I've gone back to the drawing board. These are just a bunch of spare parts at the moment."

"Actually—" Shay frowned, her gaze far away on something Nick couldn't see.

"What's wrong?" he asked, steeling himself for her criticism.

"Nothing. It's just that I was thinking—" She touched one wheel thoughtfully then looked straight at him. "Can I play inventor for a minute?"

"Be my guest." Nick stepped back, disconcerted by the way she studied him. Once he'd been able to read her thoughts so easily, but he couldn't tell what she was thinking, only that it made his stomach do a little flip and he had no idea why that was.

Shay grasped two hard, round balls from a nearby basket filled with sports paraphernalia from his youth. "Could you attach these to the wheels?"

"I suppose." Nick frowned, considering how he could do it. He turned to glance at Shay. That speculative look of hers was leading up to something. "Why?"

"Because then this machine would be exactly what your mom needs to work her hands and arms. It's a strange thing, but in the world of arthritis, moving, even though it hurts, means gaining mobility." Shay demonstrated what she wanted and waited while he attached the balls. "Yes. That's better." She tried it out. "Can you make it a little harder to move?"

Nick caught the flowery scent of Shay's perfume as he

bent to adjust the tension. Had she always smelled like the desert in bloom? "How's that?" he said, standing back, trying to regain his focus.

"It's perfect."

"We make a good team." He grinned at her.

"I didn't do anything, but you sure have a knack for inventing." Her gaze moved back to the machine he'd created for Maggie. "I wish I had something like this for another client. A boy, Ted Swan. I don't suppose…" Her head tilted to one side as she favored him with an odd look.

"No, I can't," he said when he realized she wanted him to build something else. "I don't know anything about therapy. This is just a toy."

"It's a very useful toy," she said. "You can help people with your toys."

"My field is football, Shay. That's what I intend to stick with." He felt oddly unsettled by the calculating look she gave him. She liked the machine he'd made, but if he tried to create something for this client of hers and failed, he'd look like a fool to her. He couldn't figure out why it suddenly mattered so much that Shay didn't see him as a failure; he only knew it did. "If this thing helps Maggie, great. But that's as far as I'll go."

"Okay." Her voice was quiet but her eyes brimmed with sadness. "Can you carry this inside so your mom can try it now, while I'm here?"

Nick lifted the machine they'd collaborated on. Shay led the way back to the house, her long legs easily eating up the distance from the shed. He followed more slowly, wondering about the other client she'd mentioned. It had to be a kid because that was primarily whom she worked with. He found it endearing that Shay managed to think about someone else while helping Maggie and his mom. She had always gone the extra mile for something she believed in.

But then Shay and Brianna and Jaclyn had always rushed to fill a need where they saw it, often before others even realized it was there. Zac and Kent were the same. They all pitched in whenever and however they were needed in the small community. Nick was starting to realize how much he'd missed the sense of togetherness and common purpose that Hope offered.

And how much he liked being a part of it. Maybe he'd think about something for this boy, but not till he'd finished Maggie's machine.

Inside the house, Nick stood back as Shay gently led his mother through a regimen that had her panting with effort, much to Maggie's delight.

"Hey, Grandma, we can do our exercises together," the little girl said with a grin.

"Speaking of that, we'd better get cracking with the rest of Maggie's therapy, Nick." Shay smiled at him. "I have another client to see this morning."

The rest of the time passed quickly. Shay's quiet encouragement never faltered though Maggie burst into tears at several points and Nick grew so tense he kept making mistakes.

"Don't get frustrated, Maggie. You either, Nick. You can't think of this as something you'll do and be done with. You have to practice it every day. Maggie, every morning, before you get up, I want you to do ten of those little leg lifts when you're lying in bed. Your legs will soon get used to working," Shay assured her. "But only if you keep making them do it."

"Like 'sparagus," Maggie puffed as she worked to flex her knee. "Right, Uncle Nick?"

"Right." He chuckled at her distasteful expression.

"Huh?" Shay glanced at him, her eyes questioning.

"Well," Maggie said with a deep concentration. "Grandma says 'sparagus is good for you," Maggie explained to Shay.

"Uncle Nick and I don't like it, but she said if we eat a bit every time, then we'll get to like it."

"Grandma is very smart about a whole lot of things," Nick agreed as he shared a smile with his mom. "Though maybe not 'sparagus," he whispered in Shay's ear. She turned to smile at him, a wistful look on her face. He wondered at that look, but it quickly disappeared.

Ten minutes later Shay headed out the door.

"You're doing fine," she said. "Call me if there's a problem. Otherwise I'll see you in the office next week, Maggie." With a flutter of her fingers Shay was gone, her small red convertible vanishing in a cloud of dust.

"It's like a light goes out when Shay leaves," his mother mused as she lifted her hands off the machine he'd created. "It's no wonder she was a success at modeling. How could the camera bear to look away from such inner beauty?"

His mother had always loved Shay. In high school she'd never made any bones about the fact that she liked seeing the two of them together. But Nick knew she'd always hoped something else would develop. He wasn't exactly sure how he was supposed to tell her not to hope for more than friendship. Because he couldn't offer Shay more.

A moment later she and Maggie began preparing lunch. Nick wandered out to his workshop, his thoughts on that wistful look on Shay's face when he'd teased about the asparagus. What was that about? She had looked—what? Envious?

Come on, Nick. Shay Parker, envious of you? Get real. You've got nothing she'd want.

Nick's cell phone broke into his train of thought.

"What are you doing tonight?" His friend Kent McCloy was a very busy local vet and prone to short, clipped phone calls.

"I'm guessing I'll be doing something with you," Nick shot back. "Wanna tell me what?"

"Jaclyn and Brianna have planned a housewarming for Shay. It's tonight," Kent said, sounding harried. "According to them, you, Zac and I are in charge of the food. So what are you bringing?"

Strange noises erupted in the background.

"What are you doing?" Nick asked.

"I'm waiting for a colt to make his first appearance in this world, so I can't stand here talking to you for long. Are you in, Einstein?" Kent used the old moniker he'd tagged Nick with years ago after he'd debuted his first invention.

"I'm in, Cowboy," Nick shot back, using Kent's old tag. "What do you want me to bring?"

"Some of those chocolate cookies your mom used to make the team back in high school wouldn't be hard to take," Kent said. There was a disturbance in the background. "Gotta go, Einstein. Seven at Shay's. We're going to surprise her. Bye."

A housewarming—which meant he needed to buy Shay a gift. Nick almost groaned aloud. The thought of shopping in town where everyone stopped to say hello and ask his plans now that he was out of pro ball made his stomach tighten. But he'd weather their questions today because he wanted to give Shay something special.

As he walked to the house, Nick flashed back to the night he'd visited her and the fear that had filled her eyes before she'd realized it was him at the door. Shay said she had moved back to the farm because she was trying to recreate her dad's dream, but given the way she drew back whenever he got too near, Nick now realized that dream was costing her. She'd been terrified that night, before she'd realized he was her caller.

Maybe a surprise party for Shay wasn't the best idea.

Nick dialed Kent to alert him, but his friend's phone went to voice mail. He tried Zac before recalling Zac was out of town for an all-day conference. Nick would have to think of something else.

At the sound of a neighbor's dog barking, Nick had an idea. A dog—he'd give Shay a watchdog. Nick was pretty certain her stalker didn't know where Hope was, and he was even more certain that if the man was going to make another move against Shay, he would have done it before now. But maybe having a dog would make Shay feel more secure. At least she'd have something to befriend and love with that soft heart of hers.

"Do you know if Sam Levine still has those German shepherd pups? I thought I might get one for Shay." He told his mom the plan, delighted when she offered to bake cookies and his favorite chocolate cake for the housewarming.

"I'm sure Sam has one or two left. A dog is a great idea. I believe Shay's a little nervous about being alone on the farm, though she would never admit it," his mother said, urging him to eat the bowl of soup she'd set out for lunch. "She nearly jumped a mile when I stopped out there one evening."

"When were you out there?" he asked, surprised that his mom had been to the farm.

"It was before you came home. She said there were pecans left unpicked in the orchard." His mom avoided his stare.

"Mom, I can afford to buy all the pecans you need. You don't have to go pick them." It infuriated Nick that she still acted as if she was as poor as they'd been before his success. "I'll increase the grocery budget if you need it."

"You've already spent a small fortune on us and this house." She shot him a severe look. "And I don't need more grocery money. I just wanted an excuse to talk to Shay. She misses her dad. I don't think she's had anybody to confide in for a long time. I believe she's lonely."

"I doubt that," he said in a dry tone. "Shay attracts friends like moths to a flame."

"Because she's so kind and generous." His mother paused. "You know, it sounded to me like Shay bought the place hoping she'd live there with her own family someday."

A shot of envy speared Nick in the gut.

"She's seeing someone special?" he asked, irritated that Shay hadn't told him.

"Actually I heard she broke up with someone before she came back to Hope. But she'll probably settle down soon. Shay's always been a family girl."

Somehow Nick couldn't quite wrap his mind around Shay, the world-class supermodel, being content to settle on the farm forever. That had always been her father's dream. Hadn't she been affected at all by her big city lifestyle and fancy surroundings? As he drove over to Levine's, Nick chuckled at his mom's comment. It seemed highly unlikely to him that Shay would find a suitable husband in Hope.

Or was that wishful thinking?

Nick frowned at the errant thought. Now, what made him think a thing like that? Shay was his friend. He wanted her to be happy and to have everything she wanted. He wanted her to find the man of her dreams.

Didn't he?

Shay drove slowly toward the house, puzzling over the flicker of light she thought she'd seen inside. She was imagining it, of course. There was no light. Just as there had been no one outside last night when she'd sat peering through the window at 3:00 a.m.

"You're getting weird," she murmured to herself as she turned the wheel toward the garage. "Get a grip on yourself." She breathed in and out twice, just to calm her nerves and pulled inside.

Her whole body stiffened as her headlights picked out someone standing inside the garage, on the step that led into her home. But she couldn't see who it was. Shay cringed against the seat, drawing as far back as she could. The person came down the stairs toward her but she still couldn't see their face. The light was so dim—why hadn't she put a bigger bulb in the garage? A hand reached in to touch her on the shoulder. When he moved toward her side of the car, she opened her mouth to scream but her throat sealed, stifling the sound.

Lessons from a self-defense class replayed in her head. *Fight!*

Shay pushed the car door open to pin the intruder against the wall. A moment later Nick's head appeared in her side window. "Relax. It's me." Nick pushed the door closed so he could free himself. "Shay? Sorry If I startled you."

"Of all the—what are you doing here?" Anger spilled from her like water from a burst dam. "How dare you sneak into my garage and scare the living daylights out of me—"

"Shh," he hissed. "They're inside. They'll hear you if you don't calm down."

They? Fear clung to her, but at least she wasn't alone. Shay slowly eased out of the car, overly conscious of his hand on her elbow.

"Who is inside?" she whispered.

"Everybody. Practically the whole town."

Shay frowned at him. Maybe Nick was losing it, too. She backed away, letting his hand slide off her arm, leaving the sensation of warmth where chills had been. He leaned down to rub his injured knee. "What are you doing in my garage, Nick?"

"I'm here for the housewarming, the *surprise* housewarming," he enunciated in a hushed voice. "Only I thought you might not like the surprise part so I figured I'd give you advance warning." He shot her a wounded look as he straightened his leg. "I didn't realize I'd get attacked by your car door."

"Ever hear of a phone?" Shay winced at the caustic tone in her voice. That's what fear did to you.

"I left about twenty messages. You never called me back." Nick's brown eyes flickered with frustration in the dim light of the overhead bulb.

"I shut my phone off," she remembered and blushed. "I was with a client and it kept ringing and then I forgot—I'm sorry." A housewarming? That would be Jaclyn and Brianna's idea. Warmth filled her, easing the panic that had banded her throat. She glanced down at her wrinkled work clothes and groaned. "Oh, boy. I am so not ready to party."

"They're just friends. And you look great, Shay. You always do." Nick gave her a cheering grin. "My housewarming gift to you is here." He motioned to a box on the floor in which a dark brown puppy lay curled up, fast asleep. "I wanted to give him to you before you get swamped by everyone."

"Oh, Nick." Tears welled at his thoughtfulness and the abashed way he looked at her, as if he was embarrassed by his thoughtfulness. She wanted to hug him but couldn't make herself do it. Instead she watched as he lifted the small body and cradled it in his strong arms. She reached out to touch the wiggling pup with a fingertip. "How did you know I wanted a dog?" The puppy lifted his head, licked her finger twice with his tiny pink tongue and then chewed on her a little bit. "Thank you so much, Nick. He's darling."

"He's not darling," Nick snorted in disgust. "He's a pure-bred German shepherd. He has dignity and pride and distinction!"

Nick had never been more wrong. The puppy was darling. And so was he, his big strong hands delicately caressing the tiny vulnerable ball of fur so she could check him over.

"He's so sweet." Shay laughed, pressing a kiss against a small paw. She wanted to kiss Nick, too, for his thoughtfulness. But when she looked up at him there was something in his eyes that unnerved her. It wasn't fear. It was—something she'd never seen before. Something she'd have to think about later, alone. "Thank you again, Nick."

"You're welcome. We'll have to put off further introductions until after the party though." He put the pup back in the box and laid Maggie's pink doll quilt over him to keep him warm. "That was all I could find," he muttered when their gazes met.

"Very pretty." She grinned at his aggrieved groan.

"You'd better go inside or they'll wonder what's taking you so long. I'm going to stay out here with him for a bit before I 'arrive.' I don't want anyone to know I spoiled the surprise."

"Okay." She smiled, grateful for his thoughtfulness. "It was nice of you to do this, Nick."

"Yeah, 'cause I'm such a nice guy," he mumbled, his handsome face flushed. "Go. And act surprised," Nick ordered as he backed into the shadows.

"I won't have to act," Shay whispered. She glanced at the puppy once more then unlocked her door, switched on the lights and blinked as a bunch of voices yelled, "Surprise!"

"What took you so long to come in?" Brianna demanded, grabbing her hand and leading her forward.

"I—uh, couldn't find my keys." Shay blinked at the host of people filling her home. "What's going on?"

"We're giving you a housewarming," Jaclyn said, grinning. "For once we pulled off a surprise without you guessing."

"Did you ever. Well, welcome to my home, everyone. Please be comfortable." Nick wasn't kidding—half the town *was* scattered throughout her home. She owed him big-time. If he hadn't warned her she'd have made a fool of herself in front of all of them.

Instead she'd made a fool of herself only in front of him.

She'd make it up to him later. For now she'd pretend everything was fine.

"I hope you all brought something to eat with you," she said as cheerfully as she could. "Because the fridge is empty and I'm starved."

Everyone laughed. As Shay turned, she saw Nick come in from the garage. He stood at the back of the room, his brown eyes steady as they met hers. At the thought of the way he'd taken her arm in the garage, she felt her face flush and she had to turn away.

Shay started chatting with the well-wishers who swarmed her. But she couldn't help recalling the moment when Nick's hand had rested on her arm, and she realized that the sensation had pushed away the terror that threatened to swamp her. She'd felt safe, for the first time in a long time.

And cherished.

Precious. Cared for.

Shay glanced at Nick again across the crowded room. To hide out in the garage like that just so he could take care of her…

Oh, Nick. Why can't you stay in Hope forever?

Chapter Five

"Ted says he's gonna walk by himself before I do," Maggie confided from her perch on a nearby chair the following Friday. "But I don't think he will."

"Who is Ted and what makes you think he won't?" Nick asked, glancing up from his second prototype of Maggie's roly-poly. She called it Tiger. She'd used the first one only a few times before it had broken. He'd fixed it, of course, but figured she needed a stronger machine.

"Ted's my friend," Maggie explained. "He was riding his bike and a car hit him. Shay's helping him, too."

Maggie's presence did nothing to help Nick's concentration. But he had to watch her for an hour after lunch so his mom could take a nap she desperately needed. Nick checked his watch. Ten minutes left until that hour was up.

It wasn't that he didn't enjoy spending time with Maggie. But the sooner he had this machine done, the sooner Maggie could regain her mobility, ensuring he'd make it back to Seattle in time to start his job.

"So why do you think he won't walk before you?" he asked. "Isn't this Ted kid willing to work hard?"

"He works as hard as me," Maggie assured him, her dark head bobbing. "More hard, even."

"So?" He paused and turned to look at her. "Why won't he walk before you?"

"'Cause he doesn't have a roly-poly. They're really poor 'cause his dad is sick and he can't work. Don't you think that's sad, Uncle Nick?"

"It's very sad," he agreed, checking that she hadn't yet finished sorting the box of screws he'd unearthed.

"My Sunday school teacher said we should help anyone who needs help," Maggie told him. "I wish I could help Ted."

"Yeah, me, too," Nick muttered absently. If he could make the rotating arm a fraction more pliable…

"But you *can* help Ted, Uncle Nick," Maggie crowed excitedly. "Shay and I talked about it and we know you can do it."

"You weren't supposed to tell him that yet, Maggie," Shay said from the doorway, laughter enhancing the lilt in her voice as she shook her head at the little girl. "Remember?"

"Oh. Yeah. I forgot." Maggie's face fell. "Sorry, Shay."

"Sweetie, it's okay."

Nick raised one eyebrow and scowled at her.

"Don't give me the evil eye, Einstein," she teased, her eyes sparkling. "Maggie and I were simply chatting about how Ted can't do all the exercises he should. We got talking about how the roly-poly could help him and, well, we thought how wonderful it would be if you built one for him."

"Uh-huh." Nick watched the two females share a look and sighed. "And I suppose the two of you think I should do this in my 'free' time?" he said in his drollest tone. "Which would be when, exactly?"

"I could do my exercises myself," Maggie offered. "I'm getting lots better at them."

"You are getting better, sweetie." Shay brushed back the brown strands from Maggie's face. "In fact, you're getting to be an expert. But for now you still need help."

"Let's leave sorting those screws for now, okay?" Nick

said. He lifted Maggie off the stool. "What are you doing here at this time of day, Shay? I thought you'd have appointments."

"Cancellation," she said, following him as he brought Maggie out into the sunshine. She reached up to brush her fingertips against a lemon that hung from the bottom branches of a tree he'd given to his mom in ninth grade, the year he'd spent his summer vacation working in a nursery. "I thought this would be finished bearing by now."

"It always bears late, remember? You want some lemonade?" It wasn't a question Nick needed to ask. Shay's green eyes brimmed with longing. She loved lemon anything, but she couldn't resist lemonade made from fresh lemons. "It'll cost you," he said as he set Maggie on the side of her sandbox.

"Everything costs, Nick." A haunted look flashed in Shay's eyes as she studied him. The intensity of those words and the wariness of her gaze sucker punched him. It hurt his heart to think that this was how Shay now viewed the world.

"I could use your help designing Ted's roly-poly," he said. "Unless his issues are identical to Maggie's."

"You'll do it? You'll make him a roly-poly?" A smile started at the corners of Shay's eyes and spread across her face. She stepped forward as if to hug him and then wrapped her arms around her middle instead. "Do you mean it, Nick?"

"You and Mags make it kind of hard to say no," he said, struggling not to grin at her obvious delight. Nick started plucking lemons and handing them to her.

"Don't worry. I won't be calling on your services right away because I'm at the thinking stage. I have to let the design roll around in my brain a little longer before I can begin."

"I know Ted and his family will appreciate it. So do I. And I'll be happy to help however I can. Thank you." Standing there in the sun, her arms loaded with lemons, her pink-tipped toenails peeking out from her white sandals, Shay glowed with happiness.

Something in Nick's gut gave such a wrench that he nearly jumped. *What is going on here?* He fought to get his reactions under control.

"Maggie-mine, I'm going to make some lemonade for us. Will you keep Shay company out here?" He waited for the little girl's nod then took the lemons from Shay, trying not to notice how quickly she edged away from him when her arms were empty.

Funny how much that bugged him.

It didn't take long to squeeze the fruit, add sugar, water, fresh mint and ice cubes, and carry it all outside, along with slices of the cake he'd brought home from her party.

"Oh, good! I was wishing I'd sampled this cake at my place," Shay said, sliding into a place at the picnic table, across from where he'd set Maggie. "But there was just too much food."

"You should have kept it," he said.

"If you'd left that cake at my place I'd have eaten it." She sipped her lemonade, closed her eyes and savored.

He loved watching her enjoy the cool tart drink, knowing that he'd made it for her.

"You're eating it now," Nick teased when she took a bite of her cake.

She stopped, blinked at him, her eyes wide. "Oh. Yeah." She set down her fork. The longing in her eyes made him chuckle.

"Eat the cake, Shay. You can run your six miles later."

"I'll have to. That puppy you gave me demands a lot of exercise. I named him Hugs, by the way."

"You named that masculine dog Hugs?" Nick grimaced. "Why?"

"Because he's always up for one." She munched away happily, sharing a smile with Maggie, her emerald eyes shining as she told tales of Nick's housewarming gift. "He's such a sweetie. Thank you again for giving him to me. I love him."

"I'm glad. I was told he could be trained for different things, if you want." Somehow Nick couldn't add "as a watchdog."

"I'll train him when he's older. For now I'll just love him and ignore the way he chews on my Manolo Blahnik shoes." She drained her glass then dabbed at the frothy mustache it left on her upper lip. "Your lemonade is superb, Nick. The cake was, too. Tell your mom I said thanks."

"I will." He watched her rise. "Going already?"

"I need to get back to work." She tilted her head to one side. "When would you like me to come help you in your shed later?"

"I'd be happy to have your company anytime, but actually I've had an idea about enhancements to revise the old roly-poly. I think it could be ready to try out tomorrow." He tousled the little girl's hair. "Maggie broke the original one," he teased, "but pretty soon she'll have her Tiger-version. Maybe even tonight." He winked at Maggie. "If she doesn't mind, maybe we could give the old one to Ted."

"I knew you'd help Ted, Uncle Nick." Maggie flung her arms around his neck and hugged him.

"I knew you would, too," Shay said softly.

"You did?" Nick frowned. "How?"

"Because that's the kind of guy you are. That's why your family loves you."

Nick met her gaze, and the look on her face made him want to take her in his arms. Instead, he turned his attention to Maggie.

Shay checked her watch.

"I have to go. If you bring the old roly-poly on Monday morning, we could let Ted try it. Then you could fine-tune it for his needs." She checked her watch. "I have to go. Thanks a lot, Nick."

"My pleasure."

She stopped to unlatch the fence gate just as something behind the house made a noise. Shay tensed and glanced around hurriedly, then straightened and forced a squeaky laugh. "That startled me," she said.

"Probably just mourning doves." But Nick could tell his reassurance didn't ease her anxiety. She slowly loosed her fingers, passed through the gate before she got in her car. She had to crank the ignition a couple of times to start it. Nick wasn't sure if that was Shay's fault or the car's.

"Don't you think Shay's the most nicest person in the world?" Maggie said.

"You can say 'nicest,'" Nick told her. "But I don't think 'most nicest' is grammatically correct, Maggie-mine."

"It is for Shay," the little girl declared. "She helps everybody. When I get big, I want to be just like her."

"You already are like her. You're a sweetie." Nick left her to finish her drink as he carried the dishes inside, musing on Maggie's words.

Shay *was* always trying to help people. But based on her reaction to that noise, maybe it was time for somebody to help her. Would she let him? Would he know how?

He heard Maggie talking to someone, and saw her speaking into the telephone he'd left lying on the picnic table as he headed back outside. "Who's that, sweetie?"

"Emma White's mom. Emma has casts on. Could you fix her bed so she can get in and out?" Maggie held out the phone.

Nick had to keep from rolling his eyes. With his mom, Shay and Maggie offering his services to the citizens of Hope, he wouldn't have to worry about having time on his hands. He would miss all the small-town interactions. He spared a thought to wonder who'd fix beds and other assorted issues when he returned to Seattle. *I can't worry about that,* he thought. He tousled Maggie's hair and took the phone.

Shay used the ride back to the clinic to recover her sense of equanimity, embarrassed that squabbling birds had unnerved her so badly, and that Nick had witnessed it. She had to figure out a way to get over this.

Utter frustration burned deep inside. No matter how much she steeled herself and tried not to react, she could find no way to control her panic attacks. But she could not go on living like this. Even more humiliating than freezing at the slightest noise, however, was seeing Nick's eyes brimming with sympathy. *Nick's gorgeous eyes,* she thought, before she could stop herself.

As she headed into the clinic, she realized she'd been having a number of thoughts like that about Nick lately. What exactly did *that* mean?

Just as she reached her office, Shay ran into Jaclyn. Weariness marred her friend's pretty face.

"You need to go home and rest," Shay chided.

"And you need to tell me what you were just thinking about. Whatever it was, it must have been good."

Shay blushed, and the obstetrician sank into a chair as Shay dragged forward an empty plastic box so her friend could put her feet up.

"Don't put me off, Doc." Shay frowned. "I don't need a medical degree to see you're exhausted."

"I am," Jaclyn agreed. "That's why Kent's picking me up in a few minutes. I'd planned to cook us dinner, but I think I'll ask my husband to take me out instead." She patted her baby bump. "This little one tires me out."

"You should take the advice you're always handing out to your patients and remember that having a baby is hard work," Shay scolded. Her grin faded when a rattling sound came from the front of the clinic. She checked her watch. "Aren't all the staff gone?" Dread oozed up from the pit of her stomach.

"I thought so. I'll go check it out," Jaclyn offered after a glance at Shay's white-knuckled grasp of the desk.

"No, you won't. Stay put." Shay rose, summoning her courage as she did. She walked into the hallway. "Anyone there?" she called. There was a bump, then a crash like the splintering of glass.

A band of terror tightened around Shay's throat. "We do not keep any drugs here, if that's what you're after," she said, her voice barely more than a whisper for the fear choking her words.

Who could be there? And why didn't they answer?
Oh, God, please help.

"Shay? What's wrong?" Jaclyn called. "Do you need help?"

The sound of Jaclyn getting to her feet penetrated Shay's fear. No way could she allow Jaclyn or her baby to be hurt. Shay licked her dry lips and forced out the words.

"Stay there! I'll handle this."

Her whirling stomach mocked her words. How could she handle anything when her knocking knees held her captive? The only weapon at hand was a huge medical tome sitting on a file cabinet in the hall. Shay grabbed it, swallowed hard and inched forward.

Maybe their intruder had left at the sound of their voices.

No. There was a distinct padding noise in the waiting room. Someone was still there.

With growing trepidation, Shay stepped into the front of the clinic with her book upheld. She stopped short at the sight before her. A laugh burst from her—shaky, nervous, but at least it was a laugh. She set the book down and held out her arms.

"Hello, kitty. How did you get in here?"

"I'm coming out there, Shay." Jaclyn's worried voice carried down the hall.

"Don't bother. I've caught our intruder." She cuddled the big tabby in her arms, where he seemed perfectly content to rest as she walked back to her office. "Meet our cat burglar. He broke a vase."

"Where did he come from?" Jaclyn took the cat, petting his fur.

"No clue. He must have snuck in somehow. What will we do with him?"

"I'll take him home till we find his owner," Jaclyn said. "Goodness knows we have enough space at the animal sanctuary. I hope we haven't put you out too much, Mr. Cat," she murmured dryly, smiling when he made a circle in her lap before nestling down for a rest. Jaclyn returned her scrutiny to Shay, who was making a cup of coffee. "Your hand is shaking. Are you all right?"

"It was just a bit nerve-racking. I started imagining…well, imagining a burglar in Hope is a bit silly, isn't it? I think the last time that happened here, we were in fourth grade." She turned her back, added some creamer to her coffee and took a sip, hoping it would calm her.

"You're still bothered by thoughts of your stalker, aren't you?" Jaclyn asked. "Did you talk to Brianna?"

"I did. A lot." With a sigh over the fact that she wasn't going to be able to avoid this discussion, Shay returned to her chair behind her desk. "It doesn't seem to make a difference. Something happens and boom! I freeze up."

"You didn't freeze up just now," Jaclyn said. "Did you?"

"For a minute or two." Shay realized that her stomach still hadn't settled. "I don't know why I get so freaked. I'm going along, doing fine, and then it hits me. Suddenly all I can think about is that he's returned and it will start all over again. There's not a thing I can do about it."

"You know that's not true, don't you?" Brianna said from the doorway. "Sorry—I slipped in the back door to put some stuff in my office. I didn't mean to eavesdrop."

"You know all my secrets anyway." Shay shrugged. "We're just laughing at my latest panic attack."

"No one's laughing, Shay," said Jaclyn.

"What sparked it this time?" Brianna asked.

As they related the cat story, Brianna smiled, but her eyes grew serious. "I'm worried about you, Shay. From what you've told me, it's this fear that ruined your relationship with Eric. Now it's affecting you here in Hope. Why?" She bent, kicked off her high heels and massaged her toes. "New shoes are the worst." Her focus returned to Shay. "Have you heard from the stalker guy? Is that why you're so on edge?"

"No. Nothing like that." Shay felt like a fool once again. "It's just—I know he'll be back."

"Honey, you don't *know* that. You said he hasn't bothered you since Nick threatened him," Jaclyn reasoned. "It's your fear talking."

"She's right," Brianna agreed. "You can't let this fear overwhelm you, Shay."

"I'm trying not to," she said helplessly. "But I can't seem to control it."

"That's key. Control. I've been thinking and praying about this a lot." Brianna's gaze encompassed both of them. "It seems to me, given what happened with Eric, that you've never resolved your trust issues. And you must, because this is a fight for control of your mind, Shay."

"I agree. And I think we need to pray about it." They bowed their heads, and Shay listened to each of her friends ask God to grant Shay the strength and wisdom to combat her fear.

"I appreciate your prayers," she said when they'd finished. "But why don't I feel any stronger?"

"It won't happen overnight. You must actively fight every negative thought," Brianna insisted. "Only then will you be able to finally let go. Just don't expect it to be easy. These thoughts have taken root in your mind like weeds. But you can do it."

"I hope so."

"No, Shay." Brianna shook her head. "There's no 'hope' about it. You put your trust in God. Keep your mind fixed on Him and when it strays to fear, recite Scripture to combat it."

"Which Scripture?" Shay read the Bible every day, but she'd never given a thought to reciting it like a shield.

"Last night I was thinking about you and I wrote down a few passages that have helped me in the past. Maybe they'll help you, too."

"I'm sure they will." Shay folded the paper. "You guys are the greatest. Thank you." She hugged them both, chuckling when Brianna's phone chirped a text message in a ring she recognized. "Didn't you just see Zac a few minutes ago at the school office?"

"Yes." Brianna blushed. "What can I say? We spent ten years apart. Now that we're finally married, we're making up for lost time." She winked. "We've got dinner plans tonight."

"Well, get going then," Shay urged, smiling as Brianna scrambled for her shoes, slid them on and eagerly hurried away.

"I've got to go, too," Jaclyn said. "Kent's probably waiting outside." She inclined her head. "I was looking for you after lunch, by the way. RaeAnn said you'd had a cancellation and went out?"

"Our office nurse is all-seeing, isn't she? And you're nosy," Shay teased. Jaclyn merely lifted one inquiring eyebrow. "I went to Nick's, to ask him to build one of his machines for that client you referred to me. Ted Swan."

"And did Nick agree?" Jaclyn's implacable stare was hard to ignore.

"Yes." Shay frowned. "Well, sort of."

"Sort of?"

"Well." Shay felt her cheeks warm at Jaclyn's scrutiny. "He said he'd do it if I promised to help him with it."

"Help him how?" Jaclyn eased the cat off her lap and rose.

"However I could. But before I left he said he'd had an idea to revamp the first machine he made for Maggie, which she calls a roly-poly, into something for Ted. Maggie broke that one. But I think Nick was thinking ahead and figured she'd get bored with it because he's already started something new. Maggie calls this one Tiger. You know Nick," she said. "He can't help inventing."

"I do know." Jaclyn shared a smile with her.

"Anyway, he's agreed to give the roly-poly to Ted so it seems that everything is fine." Shay grabbed her purse and followed Jaclyn, who carried the cat to the front door. "I'd be very willing to help Nick if he needs it, though."

Jaclyn looked straight at Shay, her gaze swirled with questions. Shay knew exactly what she was going to ask.

"Honey, are you feeling something for Nick?"

"Yes," Shay confessed. "Friendship, of course. Thankfulness that we've begun a kind of a renewal of the bond we shared in high school."

Jaclyn frowned. "Do you trust him?"

"Why wouldn't I trust Nick?" Shay asked.

"It's none of my business and as you mentioned, I am too nosy for my own good." Jaclyn touched her arm. "But I know you've always wanted to be married, to raise a family. And I know your panic attacks have made you wary of relationships. I just want to be sure—"

"Jaclyn, stop." Shay shook her head. "Nick's a friend. That's all. There can't be more. I freeze up if he even touches my arm. Believe me, I, better than anyone, know I'm not a candidate for another relationship. I doubt I ever will be. I've accepted that I'll stay single, and that's okay."

"I'm not sure it is okay," Jaclyn murmured, her lovely face brimming with doubt. "Just because Eric wasn't the one doesn't mean—"

"Yes, it does." Shay forced herself to sound upbeat. "Anyway, I think God meant for me to learn to stand on my own two feet. You know how hard that's always been for me, especially since Dad died. The panic attacks must be a test or something."

"I don't believe God sends fear," Jaclyn said.

"I love you for fussing, pal, but I'm going to be fine. You worry about yourself and that baby." Shay hugged her, petted the cat and pulled open the front door. "Now go have dinner with your husband and relax. That's an order, Doc."

"Yes, ma'am." Jaclyn brushed her cheek with her lips. "I love you, Shay."

"Back atcha. Now git." She stood watching as Jaclyn strode eagerly toward her husband. Kent kissed his wife, took the cat from her and stowed it in a kennel box he always carried in the back of the truck. Then he helped Jaclyn inside, waved at Shay, and the two drove off.

A rush of envy suffused Shay. Both Brianna and Jaclyn were blissfully happy in their marriages. Shay craved the love and security they enjoyed with men who treasured them and showed it. That love was something she'd seen between her parents, and it was what her father had showered on her every day of her life. She yearned for it now. But ever since Eric had told her that when she cringed from his touch it made him feel like an attacker, Shay had begun to question whether an intimate relationship was for her. She told herself that was okay, she'd settle for feeling safe.

Nick made her feel safe. But Shay was beginning to realize

that he'd be leaving soon. The only one she could depend on was herself. Jaclyn and Brianna were right. She had to deal with this apprehension that dogged her. To let it continue was to remain a prisoner.

The only question was—how would she do it?

Shay locked the office door then climbed into her car after an automatic check of the backseat. The motor didn't catch till the third try, but once it did and she was moving, she put the top down. She loved the breeze in her hair as she drove home.

The sun was beginning its colorful descent below the jagged rims of the western mountains as Shay drove into her yard. She paused outside the garage, caught up in the glory of vibrant reds, peaches and oranges that painted the horizon. Only when the scrabbling noise of an animal startled her did she realize how quickly darkness had fallen. She pulled into her garage and closed the door.

As Shay stepped out of her car, the slip of paper Jaclyn had given her with a list of verses tumbled from her pocket onto the floor. She picked it up, determined to get a handle on this fear thing starting tonight. She entered the house, then let Hugs out to run while she made dinner. Afterward, with the dishes done and Hugs curled up at her feet, she started to study the list.

God has not given us the spirit of fear; but of power, and of love, and of a sound mind.

2 Timothy 1:7.

Power, love and a sound mind—those were God's gifts to her.

It was up to her to use them.

Her thoughts strayed to Nick. He was a gift, too. A wonderful, sweet, helpful friend. But that's all he could ever be because deep down inside her secret heart, suspicion still lurked and Shay couldn't lay it to rest—not even for a wonderful man like Nick.

* * *

Nick drove the back route to Shay's, surveying every vehicle he passed, noting the driver, or, if he didn't recognize them, the kind of vehicle. It was probably obsessive and unnecessary, but Shay's face today—the panic that had filled her gorgeous emerald eyes when she'd looked at him—wouldn't leave him.

Shay wasn't a wimp or a weakling. She was a strong woman. Fresh out of high school, she'd built a career that supported her dad and herself, and then she'd found a second career when the first was no longer viable for her. She'd never been prone to flights of fancy.

But since she'd returned to Hope, he'd seen her suddenly drawing back several times. He'd heard her quick gasp when he'd touched her that day outside her office, and since then he'd taken note every time she drew away from him. He knew she was still fearful.

Though she pretended otherwise, Shay had never fully recovered from that stalking. That made Nick angry. Angry enough to ensure there was no foundation for her fears.

Nick parked his vehicle at the edge of Shay's land and walked over the perimeter, even though it was 11:00 p.m. He stood behind the leafy foliage of a paloverde tree to study her house. He had to guarantee—if only to himself—that no one was there playing tricks on her, taunting her, cashing in on her unsteady nerves.

By midnight Nick had seen nothing. But he would be back tomorrow night. Shay was a friend, and friends took care of friends.

That funny little burst of affection he'd felt for her this afternoon bubbled up again, unsettling him. He shoved it away and drove home. But back in his workshop, Nick couldn't focus on the adaptations needed on Maggie's Tiger machine.

Instead, memories of Shay cropped up, and all the things she had done for him when they were teenagers.

It was Shay who had pushed him to see himself as more than his father's son when he'd hidden his shame in this very shed after overhearing local gossip and rumors about his father. *Cal Green—you remember Cal, the no-account who'd abandoned his wife and kids for other folks to tend? That poor family, left all alone.*

Nick's fists clenched as memories of gossip and innuendo cascaded through his brain. Shay had thought his house was fun, his sisters were great, his mom the salt of the earth. In those days, whenever she'd come to his home, it was as if she suddenly came alive. The quiet introvert allowed herself to relax among his family.

That's what he wanted for Shay now—to let go of the fear that shadowed those gorgeous eyes and let joy fill her completely. He wanted to see her free and fully participating in life. That's why he'd keep making these trips at night, to make sure his friend was all right.

But friendship was Nick's only motive. It had to be, because he was Cal Green's son. Nick figured the two relationships he'd botched proved he'd inherited his dad's legacy of failure when it came to personal relations. No matter what he might or might not be feeling for Shay these days, he wouldn't risk repeating that lesson with her. Better to concentrate on loving his family to the best of his ability, and being Shay's best friend.

That would have to be enough.

Chapter Six

"That's fantastic, Ted." Shay beamed as the little boy showed off his newly learned skills, thanks to Nick's roly-poly. "My goodness, it seems like you've been working with that thing for a lot more than just a week."

"That's 'cause Uncle Nick's been helping him," Maggie chirped from the sidelines of the therapy room. "I helped, too, by cheering for him."

"Good for you, Maggie." Shay studied Nick with a smile. Despite his family obligations, and his initial refusal to take on the work, Nick still couldn't bypass an opportunity to help others when needed. She wasn't surprised. He'd always been that way.

Courtesy of a little bird named Maggie, Shay now knew that Nick had volunteered to help restore the seniors' center. He also chauffeured his mom on errands, took care of Maggie's therapy and clearly spent hours thinking of ways to help speed his niece's recovery. Yet he'd still made it a point to refine the roly-poly and help a little boy learn how to use it.

Shay's brain hummed with possibilities as she watched Nick and Ted interact. Maybe, if she went about it the right way, she could show Nick the importance of his contribution. There were so many other kids who needed someone like him to help them.

"Ta-da!" Ted completed his last feat, spread his arms wide and bowed.

"Amazing job, buddy." She wrapped Ted in a fierce hug, knowing how hard he'd struggled. "You keep working like that and soon you won't need the roly-poly."

"You mean you think he's going to walk before me?" demanded Maggie.

If Nick meant that strangled cough as cover for his laughter, it didn't work. Shay shot him a silencing look before she turned to comfort Maggie.

"It's not a contest, sweetheart," she said gently. "The goal is for both of you to walk."

"But it's my roly-poly! I don't want him to beat me!" Maggie glared at Ted as if he'd done something wrong.

Shay glanced at Nick, and she knew that making Maggie understand was up to her. So she tried reason. She tried calming words. She tried everything, but to no avail. Maggie's sour look telegraphed her irritation. Exasperated, Shay turned her glare on an amused Nick and refused to be charmed by his smile. Which, some part of her brain acknowledged, was devastating.

Funny she'd never noticed that before. Even funnier that she was noticing now, when she should be concentrating on her clients and not her client's hunky uncle.

"Do something," she growled sotto voce.

"You know, Shay, it's refreshing to know that you don't excel at absolutely everything." With a grin that took the sting out of his words, Nick knelt in front of his niece. "Listen, Mags," he began. "You offered the roly-poly to Ted. You can't take it back. That would be mean."

"But—"

"Hear me out. The important thing is that both you and

Ted walk again." He pushed the brown bangs off her forehead. "*When* you walk doesn't matter. It's like Shay said—all any of us care about is that you *do* walk again, on your own, both of you."

"But Uncle Nick," Maggie sputtered, her indignation obvious. "I started before Ted so I should walk first!"

"Sorry. That isn't how it works, kiddo." He shrugged at her mutinous look. "Be as mad as you want. All I can say is if it matters so much, then it's up to you to do something about it."

"How?" Maggie perked up, suddenly all ears.

When Nick winked at Shay she had to suppress her smile, remembering when Nick used a million coercion tactics to get his younger sisters to do something they didn't want to.

"Let's see." He pretended to think about it. "I know. Maybe you'd walk first if you worked at your exercises harder. Harder than you did this morning," he hinted, though he kept his expression neutral.

Shay watched Maggie's face color and realized that the stiffness she noticed in Maggie this past week was because Maggie had apparently sloughed off on her workouts. Shay had mistakenly attributed the slowing progress to Nick, assuming he'd become tired of pushing his niece. She'd misjudged him.

Maggie's bottom lip thrust out under her uncle's steady regard. She huffed her indignation before she turned to join Ted on a pile of exercise mats at the far corner of the room. Shay took advantage of the privacy.

"I owe you an apology," she admitted.

"Me?" Nick blinked his surprise, his bittersweet-chocolate eyes widening. "Why?"

"I assumed Maggie's lack of progress today meant you'd been slacking off. Now I realize it's Maggie who isn't putting in the effort." Shay stared straight at him. "I apologize, Nick."

For a moment his lips pinched tightly together and his

brows lowered, shielding his gaze from her. Then his frustration released in one irritated sigh.

"I am not my father," he said, enunciating in a clear, harsh tone.

Stunned by the bitterness underlying each word, Shay blustered, "I never said—"

"When I say I'll do something, I do it. You should know that about me by now, Shay."

"I do know that," she assured him, rushing to make amends. "I've always known that about you. It's not that I doubted your commitment. Not exactly." She motioned for him to sit on the nearby chair. "I guess I jumped to conclusions."

"Why? What have I done that would make you think I'd stop before Maggie has recovered her mobility?" Nick folded his long body into the chair.

"Actually, nothing," she admitted. "You've done better than I ever hoped for."

"Then why assume I'd slack off now?" The rigidity did not leave his face.

"It's not just you. Trusting isn't my strong point," she admitted. "But the way you responded when I first laid everything out, you sounded as if you could hardly wait to get away from Hope. Well, you *did,*" she said more forcefully when he raised one imperious eyebrow.

"Okay, maybe," Nick conceded. "But now your doubts about me are settled, right? You know I'm here for the duration, so you can relax."

"I do?"

"You have to know I'm not going anywhere for the next couple of weeks, for sure."

"How would I know that?" She waited for an explanation, but all she got was a cute smile that bloomed across his sun-tanned face. She ignored the giddyup of her pulse. "Tell me what's going on, Nick," she demanded.

"You know, you haven't changed all that much since we were in high school. You still can't stand it if there's something happening that you don't know about." Laughter burst from him in a great roar of amusement when she made a face.

"So what is 'happening,' as you so succinctly put it?" She wished she didn't sound so eager.

"I'm surprised somebody in town hasn't already told you, even though it's supposed to be a secret."

"I've been a little busy with work." She inclined her head. "So?"

"So I'm planning a surprise sixtieth birthday party for Mom two weeks from Saturday. The girls and their families are coming Friday evening. Saturday we'll all have breakfast together, and then in the afternoon I intend to invite the town to come help us celebrate. I'm not sure about the evening yet. Maybe we'll have a family dinner."

"It sounds fun." It had been a very long time since Shay had been part of a family event, and she felt just the tiniest bit envious. "Can I help?"

Nick slowly nodded. "Actually you can."

"Great. How?"

"I don't know if I should ask this or not." Nick's smooth forehead pleated in a frown.

"You can always ask. If I don't want to do it, I'll say no," Shay promised. "But remember, I was a kid when we moved here, and your mother became like my own. I love that woman dearly. There's not much I wouldn't do for her."

"Good to know." His eyes narrowed. "Because there's a glitch in my plans and I need some advice. I'm afraid Mom will feel like she has to be the hostess if I ask people to come to the house. I want her to be the guest of honor, to enjoy her day, not spend it waiting on other people."

Nick gazed at her intensely, and Shay started to feel strange, as if he was somehow intruding into her personal space. "Of course you do," she said, breaking eye contact with him. "Knowing your mom, you are right to be worried. She'd be rushing around, seeing to her guests, trying to make everyone comfortable."

An idea flashed in Shay's brain but she was still feeling flustered by the way Nick had been looking at her, and she couldn't seem to get her thoughts together.

"I thought maybe a reception in one of the halls in town would work, but they're already booked." Nick shook his head in frustration, but his eyes held hers, narrowed even, holding hers so that she couldn't look away. "I should have started planning earlier."

"Uh-huh." Shay found it hard to breathe under that intensity, let alone say anything halfway intelligent.

The slap of a workout mat hitting the floor startled them both. Shay and Nick blinked at each other then hurried to ensure both Maggie and Ted were all right. The kids rolled on the floor, howling with laughter, best friends once more.

Once again Nick's eyes met hers. Thankfully he spoke first, giving Shay a moment to regroup.

"Maybe I can hire some of the high school girls to act as servers or something," Nick said as he lifted Maggie. "Don't worry about it, Shay. You've got enough to do."

"Oh, I *am* going to help." Shay eased Ted onto the parallel bars. "But right now I've got to finish Ted's therapy. Can you come over to my place tonight?"

"Yeah. Sure. Okay." Nick smiled at her, which made her stomach do a funny little backflip. "I'll be there after dinner. Mom's serving asparagus, so I might even be early."

She laughed at the face he and Maggie made before they turned to leave.

Shay put Ted through his paces. He pushed himself so hard

she had to remind him that he couldn't do everything at once, even with the roly-poly.

"The secret is to work hard, but not too hard," she said as his mother rushed in looking harried.

"I'm so sorry I'm late. I agreed to decorate a cake for a friend and I had to pick up some supplies. There was a long line at the grocery store."

"No problem." After updating Susan Swan on her son's progress, Shay ruffled Ted's hair.

"No overdoing it now, Ted," she warned.

"But I want to beat Maggie." His big eyes blinked at her from his too-thin face.

"This isn't a race. Be patient. Do everything I showed you, slowly, carefully. Okay?"

His face demonstrating his frustration, Ted finally nodded. Then he and his mother left.

Since Ted was Shay's last appointment of the day, she hurried to reorganize her workout room before returning to her office. Once seated behind her desk, she let her imagination run free as she sketched out rough ideas for Nick's mom's party. By the time she leaned back in her chair to ease the crook in her neck, she was certain her plan would work. And it would be a huge surprise to the woman who always labored so hard giving to others, the woman who'd become like a mother to her.

Suddenly the ticking clock seemed overly loud in the office. Shay's nerves stretched taut as she realized she was alone. She checked her watch—almost six-thirty. Everyone had left. The eerie silence sent fear skating over her shaky nerves. Uneasiness mushroomed into anxiety.

"Don't be ridiculous," she said out loud. "There's no one here."

Though psychologically Shay knew the only danger was in her head, the rattle of a window pane against the desert wind tightened an invisible band around her dry throat and made her so skittish that all she could think was, *Get out of here!*

She grabbed her keys and her bag and hurried to the front door, only then realizing how dim the office was. One meager nightlight glowed in a losing battle to fight back the shadows of the room. She flicked on a desk lamp and immediately felt better as illumination chased away the worst of the darkness.

"Bogeymen? You're being silly," she told herself. "Go home."

Shay stepped outside and locked the door. Then she race-walked to her car. She flicked her key fob, scanned the backseat, got inside and snapped the door locks.

"Stupid habit, Shay," she mocked as she did up her seat belt. "If the guy's going to come after you again, he's certainly not going to sit in your backseat and wait for you."

She drew deep, calming breaths when the car wouldn't start. Stupid thing—she'd taken it to the garage twice this week and no one could find what was wrong yet the car still didn't start properly.

She decided to try once more before calling a tow truck. The engine finally caught. Heaving a sigh of relief, she negotiated her way through town. After a few minutes she put the top down, remembering the verses Jaclyn had given her.

God has not given us a spirit of fear.

Meaning, God wanted her to get on with her life. He certainly didn't want her skulking around, afraid of her own shadow. Afraid to be alone in the office. Afraid to trust... Nick.

Shay shoved a praise CD into the player and, once she was out of town, sang along loudly as she drove toward home. But no matter how hard she sang, she couldn't dislodge the questions that lay at the back of her mind.

A spirit of fear—about Nick? Why would she fear him? Because she'd begun to feel something for him? Because she was afraid of those feelings? Because when he came over to her house tonight he might figure out that he was becoming more than a friend to her?

Shay had found no answer to those and other questions by the time she pulled into the garage. She only knew that the fear was there. Like a cactus thorn, it had dug in deep. It would take a lot of verses to excise.

"Please help me learn to trust again," she whispered before she climbed out of the car.

Nick drove to Shay's to discuss his mom's birthday a little faster than usual, eager to talk to her. But he did savor the scenic evening drive while he wondered what brilliant idea Shay had come up with. He loved his family but was more comfortable doing the mundane stuff that needed doing. Shay was the party girl. She'd know the best way to make his mom's day special. He'd do anything to make his mom happy. No way did he want her remembering that his deadbeat dad had chosen to walk out on them on her special day. Why hadn't God given him any ideas for his mom's party?

Or any solid assurance that the job in Seattle was where he ought to be. Though it was supposed to be a sealed deal, his concern about being so far from Hope and his family gnawed at him more with every day that passed. Especially now that he realized how much his mom had come to depend on him.

That wasn't the only issue though. Nick had also begun to appreciate his time in Hope. Helping the seniors renovate the building where they'd built lifelong relationships made him covet the same sense of connection with his surroundings. And Maggie and Ted's bragging about the machines he'd made for them had brought calls from several parents who wanted him to build stuff to help their kids. Though Nick grumbled about more work, he'd appreciated Shay's efforts to scrounge old rehabilitation equipment for him to use.

The satisfaction of watching each child experiment with his unique invention surprised Nick. He loved being involved and had agreed, despite his misgivings, to let a couple of the kids' fathers help him work on the machines.

But the best part of working on those machines was the time he spent with Shay.

She made everything fun. Because of her Nick had a new appreciation for his hometown and all it offered. He hadn't really been surprised by Shay's remark that she'd love to raise her own family here. She was so caring and generous—she'd make a great mom.

And working with Shay and her kids had shown Nick fathers who gladly got involved in their kids' lives, men totally unlike his dad. These guys were wholly vested in seeing their kids thrive and offered to help on their weekends off or until late at night if Nick needed them. When it came to their kids, these dads were totally unselfish.

Was that what had sparked his own desire to know what being a father would be like? Would he be a better dad than his own had been to him? Could he love and guide his own son or daughter better than his father had?

Yet each time Nick dared dream that, the vision was snuffed out by bitter memories of his last meeting with his father. He'd thought a reunion might work but his father's rejection of him, his sisters and his mom showed Nick how silly it was to imagine he, the son of a man so uncaring, would be any different. Hadn't he already messed up twice? What had changed?

Nothing. Nick wouldn't risk another relationship. He certainly wouldn't involve a child in his failures. That's why his own dreams had to be suppressed to allow him to fulfill his primary duty—to care for his family.

As if to emphasize that, his cell phone rang. It was his sister Cara.

"I'm so sorry the twins aren't feeling well, sis," Nick said after she'd revealed her doubts about making the drive for the party. "But they'll be over this bug soon, won't they? You guys can't miss out on Mom's special day."

"I don't want to miss it, Nick, but driving four hundred miles with the twins is going to tax all of us." He heard the hesitation before she said, "Besides, I'm not so sure bringing my kids would be good for Mom. She'll already be ramped up. The twins don't sleep through the night yet and the noise they make will prevent Mom from getting the rest she needs. Maybe we should come later, when the fuss has died down."

"No way, Cara. You can't miss this party. And Mom will be hurt if you and the munchkins aren't there." He thought for a moment. "Why don't all of you fly into Las Cruces? I'll pick you up. The tickets will be my treat," he insisted, knowing Cara and her husband couldn't afford the expense. "We'll get you a hotel room if need be. We'll figure it out."

"Nick, that's too much—"

He cut off her interruption. "Just come and enjoy yourself. I've got it all taken care of."

As Nick said goodbye and pulled into Shay's driveway, he hoped Shay would help make his words would come true. A minute ago he'd been regretting that he had to leave Hope, but here was another reason for showing up for that assistant coaching job—his family needed him. Without a steady job he'd run out of funds to pay for things like spur-of-the-moment plane tickets. Then he'd be as useless to his family as his father. Leaving Hope for that job was the right choice and he needed to stop doubting his decision.

Nick climbed out of his truck and blinked in surprise. Shay had all the outside lights on—every single one of them. Something must be wrong.

He strode to the front door and rapped once, hard, before he called out, "Shay? It's me."

She opened the door a few seconds later, struggling to hold back the madly wriggling puppy. Her laughter bubbled out to greet him, eliminating his worry. Despite her efforts, Hugs burst free of her grip and in one giant leap had his front paws on Nick.

"Hey, guy. What's got you so excited?" Nick squatted to pet the animal. When the dog had calmed, he rose and shook his head. "Giving you this fellow may have been a mistake," he muttered, swiping his thoroughly licked face with a tissue.

Shay brushed off her jeans. "He gets a little—exuberant. That's all."

"Exuberant? That's one word for it." He was about to pull the outside door closed when Shay stopped him by laying her hand on his, for one tiny second. Then she pulled it away. "What?"

"Don't close the door. We're going out again. I need to show you something."

She didn't sound scared, he noted with relief. She sounded sort of—keyed up.

"Is anything wrong?" He searched her face for the fear he often saw buried in those beautiful eyes.

"Just—come with me. Wait. I need my shoes." She thrust her pink-tipped toes into the rattiest pair of sneakers he'd ever seen. The shoes did go with her worn, almost threadbare jeans and the chunky, red-checked flannel shirt with holes in the elbows. Swaying pigtails made the picture complete. Nick smirked. Supermodel indeed.

And yet, even in work clothes, there was something exquisitely elegant about Shay, something that made him want to protect her.

"Okay, let's go." The dog bounded out in front of them. Nick went next, waiting while Shay locked the door behind her.

"Is that really necessary?" he asked as she pocketed the key.

"Let's say, I'm not sure that it's not. Come on." She avoided his stare by leading the way to the harvest shed. Once there, she unlocked the big double doors and threw them wide. "Well, what do you think?" Shay was so keyed up her copper curls almost vibrated with anticipation. She danced from one foot to the other, eyes wide and expectant. When he didn't immediately answer, she looked at him as if he'd become particularly slow-witted. "For the party, of course."

Nick took in the room, touched that Shay had wanted to offer her home for his mother's celebration. For a moment, he couldn't speak.

"Think of the advantages," she continued. "There's plenty of room to park in the yard, space for people to spread out, shelter if the sun gets too strong, and best of all, it's easy to decorate."

Nick studied the big shed, his nose twitching at the aroma of past pecan harvests. It was clean, rustic and, best of all, not too fussy—his mother would definitely approve.

"There's a company in Las Cruces that rents those big white tents. We could get one for that side." She glanced at him, waiting for his nod before she continued. "A band could set up over there. There are a couple of local bands that play country music—your mom loves country music," she reminded. "There'd be lots of room over here if folks wanted to dance."

Nick hadn't seen Shay so vivacious in years. Her skin bloomed a rosy peach. Her green eyes, lit by the gigantic yard light, radiated pleasure and eager anticipation. She was the most beautiful woman he'd ever seen.

Ever.

"You don't like it." In a flash, her delight snuffed out. "I'm sorry. I thought—"

"It's perfect," Nick said. And it was. His mom was going to love it.

"You don't have to say that. It was just an idea." She turned away.

"I'm not just saying it." He stopped her with a hand on her arm. Though she drew away from his touch, Nick wouldn't let her escape so easily. He grasped her fingers in his and hung on until she faced him. "I think it's absolutely brilliant, Shay. But it's a lot of work. Are you sure you want to take this on?"

Shay looked down at their entwined hands, and for a moment Nick thought he saw her smile at the sight. And then she slowly pulled her hand from his.

"Are you kidding? I'd love a chance to make the old place come alive with a party. Dad always said we had the best land for partying."

Nick almost laughed as that glimmer of pure joy flared to life in her eyes again.

"The stove is old, but it still works. So does the fridge. We've got enough power out here to make coffee, string fairy lights and whatever else we dream up." She continued, listing one asset after another until she ran out of breath.

"You've done some serious thinking about this." Her generosity amazed him, but then, that was Shay. "There's only one thing." Nick had to say it before she went any further. "What about Maggie? Will she be able to handle it out here?"

Shay looked at him. He could tell she was now considering all the aspects of the day from his niece's viewpoint. She was silent so long it made him nervous.

"Well?" he demanded when he couldn't wait any longer.

"I don't know." Shay's mouth stretched in a smile. "But we can find out."

"How?"

"Tomorrow you bring Maggie out here for her session and we'll see how she adapts." She chuckled when he blinked in surprise.

"Seriously? You want to do this?" He wasn't sure about it—it seemed a lot to ask. But nothing else he'd come up with came even close to Shay's plan.

"Absolutely serious." She grinned at him as if he'd given her the biggest gift anyone could. "Let's go back to the house. There are a lot of things to discuss." She tugged him along beside her as she talked. "For one thing we'll need tables and chairs…"

As Shay talked, Nick wondered if she realized she was touching him. Apparently she hadn't because halfway to the house, she yanked her hand from his arm as if she'd been scalded.

"Sorry," she mumbled. "I didn't mean to drag you."

"Hey, what are friends for?" He changed the subject before she could get more flustered. "Do you think we could wrangle a campfire? Your dad used to have an old tractor wheel we used when we held our youth group out here. Is it still around?"

"Yes! I saw it in those bushes where the barn used to sit." Shay skipped up the stairs with the dog nipping at her heels. She motioned Nick to follow her inside. "I've got iced tea. I think it's probably too sweet but—"

"The sweeter the better," Nick told her, thinking that Shay looked very sweet as she bustled around to offer him some cinnamon buns she'd made to go with the tea.

"They're your mom's recipe," she said.

"When do you find time to make cinnamon buns?" he asked.

"I couldn't sleep last night so I baked." Before he could ask her why, she handed him a filled tray. "Come on."

Though he wanted to say more, Nick followed her to the table in front of the wall of windows. She took his tray and set it on the table, beckoned him to a chair then folded herself onto the floor in what he'd once heard termed the Lotus position.

As Nick munched his cinnamon bun and sipped his tea, he couldn't help but think how he felt completely comfortable in Shay's home, sharing her baking and talking about his mom's party and what would happen next week, next month. Gradually his worries about the party seeped away. Shay's place was far homier than his condo and Nick had a hunch the exterior would soon boast that same relaxed, beckoning feel she'd created inside.

Too bad he wouldn't get to see what she did with the place.

He'd be in Seattle.

Alone.

Chapter Seven

"I can't do it, Shay. I can't!"

Maggie's mournful wail pierced Shay's heart. Everything for Mrs. Green's birthday was coming together so perfectly. But if Maggie couldn't manage the rough terrain around Shay's pecan shed with her braces and her Tiger machine, they couldn't have a party for her grandmother here.

Shay glanced at Nick and saw her worries reflected in his eyes. If Maggie couldn't handle the ground, their party plans has just flown out the window.

Nick sighed and nodded. "Okay then."

"But I'll practice lots, really I will," Maggie promised Nick as tears streamed down her cheeks. "I don't want to miss the party, Uncle Nick."

"Whatever happens, you are *not* staying home from your Grandma's party, Maggie-mine." Nick hunkered down until he was at her eye level. "No way."

"Do you promise?" she asked with a sniff.

"Cross my heart." He brushed away her tears with the tenderest of touches then gently set her on a nearby stump. "Here's the deal. You keep working your hardest. Don't say a word to Grandma about her party. I'll think about this some more. So will Shay. Okay, darlin'?"

"Okay." Maggie huffed a huge sigh of relief, which turned into a giggle when Hugs jumped into her lap. She obviously trusted her uncle to sort everything out. But from the way Nick looked at Shay, she knew he was as stumped as she was.

"Maybe we should go with the wheelchair," she suggested, hating the very idea of it.

"After all the work she's put in to get herself walking?" He shook his head, his gaze on something distant as he turned over the problem in his mind. "No way. A wheelchair would be no better in this gravelly sand anyway."

"Well, we have to come up with something." Frustration at the seeming hopelessness of the situation gnawed at her. "Maybe a new machine?"

"I haven't got time to design and build another machine before Mom's party!" he exclaimed, eyes widening. "Even if I had a clue what to build, which I don't."

"Then we're back at square one." Shay bit her bottom lip as she checked her watch. "I have to get back to the office."

"You go ahead." Nick sighed as he raked a hand through his already mussed hair. "Maggie and I have to pick up Mom at the hairdresser's. Thanks anyway."

"I'm not giving up yet, Nick, and don't you either." For a second, Shay felt tempted to reach out and reassure Nick with a touch. Startled by her impulse, she offered him a smile instead. "Your mother deserves the best party we can put together for her. With Maggie present."

"Hey, Uncle Nick and Shay," Maggie called. When they walked to her side, she tilted her chin and stared at them.

"What's the matter, honey?" Shay touched her cheek. "Do you hurt?"

"No. But do you remember last Sunday when Pastor Marty said God wants us to talk to Him about the hard stuff *and* the easy stuff? This is really hard. I'm gonna pray for God to help me walk for Grandma's birthday."

"That's the spirit, Mags." Nick hugged her and pressed a kiss against the top of her head. He scooped Hugs from her and handed the wriggling bundle to Shay then swung Maggie into his arms. "Now, come on. You and I need to let Shay get back to work."

"Okay. Bye, Shay." Maggie wagged her fingers at Shay then blew a kiss.

"Bye, sweetie." Shay caught the kiss in her outstretched palm and blew one back. She laughed when Nick reached in front of Maggie and caught it. After pretending to swoon, he tucked his clenched hand to his heart mimicking his performance of Romeo in their high school play. "That kiss was for Maggie," she chided, laughing again when he pretended to pout. Nick was just so much fun. What would she do when he left?

Shay walked over and brushed her lips against Maggie's forehead. "Don't give up."

"I won't." Maggie's brown eyes shone. "I'll pray about it when she's not listening."

Shay watched them drive away, waving until she couldn't see them anymore, then returned to the house just as the phone rang.

"Hello?"

No one answered.

Immediately, memories of the innumerable calls she'd answered with the same result swamped her.

Is it him? Is he back?

Fear crept up her backbone as she laid the phone down.

God has not given us a spirit of fear.

Shay repeated the words, but before peace could fill her soul, the phone rang again. She wiped her damp palms against her thighs, and then picked up the receiver a second time.

"H-hello?"

Nothing. No dial tone. No voice. Just an empty yawning silence.

"Who is this?" she whispered.

Click.

God, help. The fingers of fear clamped hard around her throat. *Not a spirit of fear,* her brain chanted. But it seemed her heart didn't get the message because when the phone's shrill peal broke the silence for the third time, it took every ounce of courage Shay had to answer it.

"Shay? Shay, are you there? Oh, this stupid cell phone. Three times I've dialed this number and I still can't hear if anyone is answering. I should have let Nick get me a new one and tossed this dumb thing in the garbage. Doris, do you know how I tell if this thing is working?"

Nick's mother. It was Nick's mother calling.

Shay's throat suddenly opened.

"Mrs. Green, this is Shay. Can I help you with something?"

"Oh, good. You're there." She let out a huff of irritation. "Nick said he was driving out to talk to you while I was getting my hair cut. I wanted to tell him to pick me up at the grocery store, but I can't reach his cell phone."

"He's already left, Mrs. Green. I'm sorry." Shay smiled at the hiss of irritation. "But I'm sure if you leave a message with Doris, she'll pass it on to Nick." The town's hairdresser had an uncanny knack for being able to relate most messages before the telephone did.

"Oh, yes, I know that, dear. It's just that I was hoping to get him to look at Faye Campbell's granddaughter's old tricycle on the way. Faye's throwing it out. I thought he might be able to adapt it somehow for Maggie. Faye says it has special tires that work in any conditions. With all the gravel in my yard, I thought…"

The rest of Mrs. Green's sentence disappeared into oblivion as Shay registered what she'd said. Special tires—

"Shay? Are you there? Oh, this stupid phone." The line went dead.

Shay hung up and tried call return but Mrs. Green's number was busy. Faye Campbell. She'd said Faye Campbell had this tricycle.

Shay patted Hugs, grabbed her car keys and left, glad for once the car started without a problem. Maybe she could catch Nick on the road to town. When she reached town without seeing his truck, she dialed the office and asked RaeAnn for directions to Mrs. Campbell's.

"Your next client is here," RaeAnn warned.

"I'll be a bit late, but I'll be there," Shay promised.

When Shay pulled up in front of Faye Campbell's big Victorian home, she saw a pile of discarded things, obviously waiting for trash pickup. But it was the big tricycle that snagged Shay's attention. The wheels were not like the usual bicycle tires. They were the old-fashioned very wide kind— Was this the answer she'd been praying for? She hopped out of her car and rang the doorbell.

It took a bit of convincing but Shay finally persuaded the older woman to allow her to store the tricycle in the side yard until Nick could pick it up. She'd no sooner disentangled it from the other items when a truck pulled up and two men began loading the junk into the back.

"Want us to take that, too?" one of them asked.

"No, thanks. I've got an idea for this," Shay told them.

"A project, huh?" The burly driver surveyed the rusted fenders, torn leather seat and bent handlebars. "Good luck. You'll need it."

"Thanks." Shay pushed her treasure to the area under a big cottonwood tree where Mrs. Campbell had directed. "Thank you very much," Shay told her. "I'll have it out of here by tonight."

"As long as it's gone when I get back, I'll be happy," Mrs. Campbell said.

Shay said goodbye and got back in her car, her heart light. That was a heavenly answer, wasn't it? Surely a clever guy like Nick could figure out how to make those big tires work. He had to. Nick was pouring his heart and soul into this party so his mom would have a wonderful day. Shay was going to do everything she could to make sure the day was absolutely perfect.

For Mrs. Green, of course.

But also for Nick. Her very dear friend Nick.

Because she wanted to see Nick happy.

What could be wrong with that?

Saturday, the morning of his mom's birthday, Nick stood outside the doors of Whispering Hope Clinic, anxiously shifting from one foot to the other. Getting the wheels on Maggie's Tiger was supposed to be the hard part. He'd managed that without any problem. But this—this had him panicked.

On the phone Shay had promised she'd meet him here in five minutes. So where was she?

"Nick? What's so urgent?" came her voice from behind him, gilded with laughter. "And what's that on your pants?"

He twisted to get a better look at his backside and groaned. "It figures."

"It looks like—icing?" Shay frowned. Then her eyes widened. "Your mom's birthday cake…?"

"…is now mush," he finished, trying not to grit his teeth.

"Because?" She waited for his explanation, but her gaze slid back to the icing.

"Because some kid went racing through a stop sign. I hit the brakes to avoid him and the cake—well, it flew all over the place." Nick grimaced. "Trust me when I tell you there is no way to salvage any of it for this afternoon."

"I see." She arched one eyebrow, but he caught the flicker of a smile at the corner of her mouth.

"This is not funny," he barked.

"Yes, it is. Kind of." She giggled as she reached up and touched the top of his head, then showed him the pink icing on her finger. "You're wearing a lot of this cake."

"What am I supposed to do, Shay?" He realized his entire right sleeve was also plastered with mashed cake and icing. "I checked with the bakery. They don't have another cake that big, or anything close to it. I also checked the grocery store. No big cakes. Just a ton of little round ones. Buddy Simms is pretty mad. Their delivery got doubled or something."

"Cupcakes?" Shay asked, her green gaze narrowing.

"I guess that's what you call them." He waited impatiently. Shay had come up with the answers to so many other issues—was it expecting too much to think she could solve this, too? He watched as she pondered the dilemma while he found himself pondering just how beautiful she was. He caught himself—now was not the time.

"Go and buy them," she said.

"Buy the cupcakes?" He frowned. "How many?"

"We guessed there'd be over a hundred people to come for your mom's party, but yesterday Heddy Grange said there will probably be more like two hundred."

Heddy Grange knew everything about everyone in Hope. If she said they'd have a full house—well, he wasn't going to argue.

"How many does the store have?" Shay asked.

"I think he said—maybe around six hundred?" Nick frowned. "I can't remember. Apparently they always order a bunch for some school event, but the company shipped way too many. Buddy told me he was going to freeze the overage until the truck comes back next week."

"Maybe he won't have to." Shay tilted her head to one side,

her copper hair shining in the sun. "Maybe he'll give you a deal, just to be rid of them."

"But they don't have any icing or decorations," Nick sputtered. "Why do we want a bunch of plain little cakes?" This was not the solution he'd hoped for.

"Never mind that. Just go over there and buy them. Tell him I'll pick them up in twenty minutes. After that," she said, pushing his shoulder, "go join your family for breakfast at the restaurant. I've got an idea."

"You always seem to have an idea." He had to smile. "Bike wheels, birthday parties, cake messes. The mind boggles."

"Don't worry, Nick. It will be fine." She was scanning numbers on her phone. "If there are leftovers, you can take them to coffee time at church tomorrow morning."

Somehow, Nick knew Shay would handle it. Again he was struck by how much he was willing to put his trust in her when he wouldn't have afforded anyone else the same, especially if it involved his family.

"Sure you don't want help?" he asked. "I feel like I'm dumping this in your lap and running."

"You are dumping it in my lap," she teased. "But at least there's no icing on me. Yet." She laughed when he groaned. "Anyway, I'll have help—Brianna and Jaclyn are at my place now with Zac and Kent. I came to pick up the coffee I bought yesterday and left in my office. Everything's under control. You go enjoy your sisters and their families."

"Okay."

"You might want to wash some of that icing off first, though. Your mom might guess about the cake."

"I owe you, Shay," Nick told her sincerely. "Big-time."

"And I intend to collect soon. But that day is not today." She waved at him. He started to walk away but then she called him back.

"Yes?"

"Maggie?" she asked, her beautiful face telegraphing her anxiety.

"Will be moving around like a hummingbird searching for flowers," he told her. Nick cupped her cheek in his palm, loving her for her concern about his niece. How could one woman have such a generous heart? How lucky was he to have her in his life? "For now, and that is thanks to you and that tricycle. But Mags wants to surprise you, so I can say no more."

Shay's eyes sparkled. "That little girl has got the faith of a giant. And the heart of a champion. Just like her uncle."

"Then we're in good company," he said, brushing the end of Shay's nose with a fingertip of icing. His heart felt huge in his chest. Shay Parker thought he had heart. What a compliment. He hoped she'd never think less of him.

When she didn't immediately back away from his touch, Nick's heart rate accelerated until he could barely breathe. Could that be because she wasn't afraid of him anymore? He checked her eyes and found no fear lurking there. That made him want to hold her close and reassure her that he'd always be there for her.

Only—he wouldn't be.

So all he said was, "Later."

Nick headed to his car, fully aware that he would never be able to get enough of the icing and cake off his clothes for his family not to suspect something was amiss. Well, let them suspect. He wasn't going to explain. This was his mom's day, and nothing was going to ruin it.

Thank heaven for Shay. As Nick drove away, he saw her talking on her phone a mile a minute wildly gesticulating. Before he turned the corner, he watched her hesitantly peek into the rear of her car before climbing in.

So Shay wasn't afraid of him, but she was still afraid of something. Nick made a decision. He was going to help her let go of the past and move into the future. No way could he let that beautiful woman who held such a special place in his heart suffer any longer. It was time for Shay to embrace life, and he was going to help her do it.

He owed her at least that much.

Shay watched as Nick led his mother to the table where the cupcakes were assembled into a beautifully decorated birthday display.

"I can't thank you enough, Susan," she murmured to Ted's mom. "You've made them look so beautiful—far better than the ordinary cake we had planned. A lot of people are going to ask who made that masterpiece."

"I'd be happy to get another job," Susan said. "I used to work in a bakery. It's something I really enjoy."

"You're certainly good at it," Shay said.

Nick's stunned surprise on seeing the cupcake cake was gratification enough. The "thank you" he now mouthed at Shay was, well, icing on the cake. A quiver that started in her stomach moved up to hug her heart. Did he know she'd do almost anything for him?

"I'd better get home. Ted's with his dad. They probably both need rescuing." Susan's eyes widened when she saw the check Shay handed her.

"This party wouldn't have been the same without a cake. Thank you." Shay smiled as the grateful woman left, thinking she'd be sure to mention Susan's name this afternoon. Maybe she could help Ted's mom get more work. The woman was talented, and it had to be tough for her to manage on part-time cleaning wages and her husband's disability check.

When Nick led everyone in a slightly off-key rendition of "Happy Birthday," Shay joined in, clapping with everyone else as Mrs. Green made a vigorous effort to blow out the relighting candles Nick had chosen. Then Shay motioned to the girls from the cheerleading squad, who'd agreed to act as servers, to begin handing guests a beverage.

A sweet sense of satisfaction blossomed deep inside Shay as she noted how easily people mingled through the yard, enjoying the food and the company. A local group—old friends of Nick's sister Cara—played music that soon drew a few dancers. The babble of conversation and Mrs. Green's glowing face proclaimed this party a total success.

Kids squealed and giggled nearby as they jumped and bounced inside the blow-up castle Nick had rented. But it was Maggie who caught Shay's eye.

Shay knew Nick had attached the wheels from Mrs. Campbell's tricycle to Maggie's Tiger machine, but how he'd done it so successfully was a mystery. Maggie moved freely over the gravelly ground, captivating everyone with her bubbling laughter.

"The party's a success, isn't it?" Nick murmured in her ear a few minutes later.

"It certainly is," she agreed. There was that quiver again and the rush of warmth to her heart that Nick always brought.

"It's because of you, Shay." Nick's dark gaze held hers. "None of this could have happened without you. I don't know how to thank you."

"Are you kidding?" She shook her head. "You were the driving force. Anyway, look at your mom's face. That's all the thanks I need."

"Me, too."

They stood together, watching Mrs. Green hand out cupcakes to her friends. The fatigue of the previous day had vanished, leaving a carefree woman who interacted with each grandchild who rushed up for a hug before disappearing back inside the jumping castle.

"Excuse me, Shay," Brianna said. "Hey, Nick. Great party."

"That's Shay's doing," he answered, smiling at Brianna.

Brianna turned to look at Shay and gave her a wink that made Shay blush a little.

"I just wanted to let you know, Shay. We're running a bit low on coffee and I can't find any more grounds," Brianna said. "So I'm going to take a run into town."

"I'll do it. I'm the one who miscalculated." Nick dug his keys out of his pocket. "I guess I'm not very good at planning for parties."

"Everyone here thinks you're great at it. Including me." Shay grinned at him. "And you didn't miscalculate. There's lots of coffee. I just forgot to take it out of my car after we finished unloading those cupcakes. I'll go get it."

"I'll join you in a sec," Brianna said. "First I want to ask Zac to put together those treat bags Jaclyn and I plan to give the kids later."

"Great idea." Shay touched Nick's arm to gain his attention. She waited for the usual sense of panic and realized with surprise that it wasn't as strong as usual. "Maybe you and your sisters could take over passing out the cupcakes and give your mom a rest. She's scrunching up her hand as if it's sore."

"Really?" Nick took a quick look at his mom then faced Shay again. "Don't miss a thing, do you?" For a moment, Nick stood there, looking down at her as if there were something else he wanted to say, but after a moment he seemed to change his mind. "Thanks. Again," was all he said.

"You're welcome." As she walked back toward the house, Shay felt a surge of satisfaction. The party was everything she'd wanted for Mrs. Green. Maggie was as mobile as possible. The day was sunny and warm without being stifling. And Nick—Nick was happier than she'd seen him in a long, long time.

"Thank You for answering Maggie's prayers," she whispered. "And mine."

It felt odd to walk inside her house without unlocking

the door, but there was no way to keep the house locked up when so many people needed access. She walked through the kitchen, trying to ignore the chaos. The place would need a good cleaning when the party was over, but a little mess was well worth the amount of joy the party had brought. She opened the garage door to get the coffee out of her trunk and flicked the light switch. With a flash the bulb burnt out.

"Great timing," she grumbled. Shay grabbed for the flashlight she kept hanging by the door for just such emergencies. Then she remembered leaving it in the pecan shed last night. "Oh, for goodness' sake," she muttered in exasperation as she hesitated. "Just get the coffee out of the car, Shay."

Her voice sounded shaky in her own ears. Suppressing her disquiet over the darkness, she felt her way along the car's fender until she found the door. She opened it and reached inside, flicking the trunk switch. At least the interior car light provided a little illumination.

The quiet snick of the trunk lock releasing did not drown out the rustle of something behind the car.

Shay froze.

"Is someone there?" she asked, peering into the shadows.

Nothing. And then it came again, a sound that was like shuffling footsteps.

"Who's there?"

No answer.

The ominous dread of knowing someone lurked in the shadows made Shay's knees knock. As she cowered in the semidarkness, she tried to remember the verses she'd read.

But all she could think of was, *Please, God, send Nick.*

Chapter Eight

"Have you seen Shay?" Nick asked Brianna.

"No, and we're getting really low on coffee." Brianna frowned. "I'll go check on her."

"I'll go. You finish the kids' bags," he told her with a wink. "Your work is much prettier than what my feeble attempts would produce."

Waylaid by several people on his way to Shay's house, Nick took longer than he intended to get there. His concerns ballooned when he didn't find her in the kitchen.

"Shay?" Her name had barely left his lips when he noticed the door to the garage standing ajar. He reached for the doorknob then paused when he heard a soft whimper. "Are you in here, Shay?" No answer. Then he saw her.

The dim glow of the car's interior lights made Shay a ghostly figure as she huddled on the hood of her car, hugging herself. Nick spotted a switch on the far side of the wall. He negotiated his way over, flicked it upward and then pushed the door opener. As the garage door slid up and daylight flooded the space, he hurried back to her.

"Shay, what's the matter?" he asked. He had to repeat himself twice, until finally she lifted her head.

"Someone's there," she croaked in a hoarse voice. "Behind the car." Her emerald eyes stretched wide with terror.

Nick glanced over one shoulder. "I don't see anyone."

"They were there," she insisted. A shudder made her body tremble. "I heard someone."

"Okay, I'll check." Nick walked around the car to see a plastic bag caught in the door hinge rustling as the wind toyed with it. He grabbed it and returned to stand beside her. "It was just a bag. It must have caught in the door from all that wind last evening. You're safe, Shay."

Her glazed green pupils gradually narrowed into focus. "A b-bag? That's it?"

"That's it. There's nothing else there, Shay. I promise. Come on." Nick held out a helping hand as she slid off the hood of her car. Her fingers clung to his. Nick had no intention of letting go. For the first time since New York Shay needed him and it felt good to be able to be there for her when she'd done so much to help him.

Maybe it felt too good?

It was great she'd begun to trust him. But who would be there to help after he'd gone back to Seattle? The realization that he might not be there when Shay needed him most made Nick clasp her hand that much tighter.

"I feel so s-stupid," she stuttered, avoiding his gaze.

"You aren't stupid." She was shaking. Nick wrapped his arms around her and held her. "You got spooked. It can happen to anyone."

"Sure it can." She inhaled then pulled away from him. "Does it happen to you?" she demanded, her green eyes furious. She strode up the stairs into her house. "What an idiot I am."

"You're not." He followed her then suddenly stopped. "Shay?"

"Yes?" She turned.

Her beautiful face was so pale. Nick's breathing hitched at the pain he saw. He wanted to hold her until the fear dissipated. He wanted to comfort her. But he knew she'd pull away. All he could do right now was give her some space and be there if she needed him.

"Didn't you come out here for the coffee?" he asked.

"Oh. Yes, I did. It's in the trunk." She scurried inside.

Her distress gutted him. To see her so shaken—well, Nick was grateful for this small reprieve to regain his equanimity. He retrieved the cans of coffee then followed her into the kitchen. When she saw him, she reached for the doorknob. Her hand was trembling, and she knew he'd seen it. But she pretended all was normal.

"I hope no one's gone thirsty." The tremble in her self-conscious laugh gave her away.

"I doubt it. We've only been away a few minutes." Nick frowned.

"Oh." She inhaled deeply. "Good."

"Listen, Shay, you should get the light switch moved over beside the house door. It's not a good thing to go out there in the dark," he said quietly. "A rattler could have gotten in, and they don't like being disturbed."

"It's the one mistake the contractor made that I haven't rectified," she agreed. "I had the hall light on when I went out. It didn't seem that dark then." She visibly struggled to keep her tone even. "Besides, I always close the garage door as soon as I drive in. A snake couldn't get in that fast."

"You were never afraid of rattlers anyway." Nick suddenly recalled a high school biology presentation she'd made about handling dangerous snakes. It had included a hands-on demonstration. "Snakes don't bother you, but people do," he said half-jokingly.

"Totally irrational, isn't it?" Chin thrust forward, she headed out the door and walked toward the party.

"Nobody ever said fear was rational."

Shay didn't answer. Nick touched her arm, and she jerked away.

"Talk to me, Shay," he begged. "You thought your stalker was back, didn't you?"

"It's—Nick, I'm fine. I just let my panic get out of control."

Or you lost control. But Nick didn't say that as Shay turned away.

As he walked beside her back to the birthday party, which was still going full swing, his gut roiled at his powerlessness to help her. Beautiful Shay Parker had gone above and beyond for him, for his mom, for Maggie and for the community of Hope. But inside she suffered terribly. She'd tried to hide her fear from him but he'd seen it in those beautiful eyes, and it stabbed him with a fierce anger every single time.

Why? he demanded of God. *Why does Shay have to go through this?*

Nick hated the image of Shay cowering on her car, hunched over, afraid. He wanted to set her free, to see the old Shay return, laughing, copper curls tossed back, wide open to everything life sent her way.

Can't You help me, God? She's such a special woman, a very special friend.

Like an echo, a question came into his mind.

Friend? Is friendship all you want from Shay?

"I don't know how to thank you, dear." Mrs. Green enfolded Shay in a tight hug. "Today was simply fantastic."

"I'm glad." Shay basked in the love she felt emanating from Nick's mother. Mrs. Green always made her feel as if she was a favored daughter. "I was thrilled Nick allowed me to help out with your party."

She helped the weary woman ease into a lawn chair then sank into the one beside her. Brianna and Jaclyn had banished Shay from the kitchen for cleanup while their husbands disassembled the tables.

The Green girls chattered together as they picked up the refuse left from Chinese buffet Shay had provided for the family dinner. Maggie and the other kids were grouped around Nick. In the glow of the campfire, each child's eyes expanded as they leaned forward to hear every sensational detail of the story he was telling them.

The perfect ending to a perfect day, Shay mused. The growing dusk seemed to invite introspection.

"Which part of today did you enjoy the most?" she asked.

"I appreciated every moment, dear. But do you know why this particular birthday you helped me celebrate is such a blessing?"

"No." Shay frowned. Nick hadn't said a word.

Mrs. Green smiled. "Years ago my husband left us on my birthday," she murmured. "I was devastated."

"Of course you were." Shay clasped her gnarled hand, smoothing the knotted knuckles with her fingers. Mrs. Green hadn't given a sign that she had bad memories or was less than blissfully happy today. "I can't imagine how upsetting it must be to face that every year on your special day. All this time—how did you manage?"

"I didn't at first." Nick's mom chuckled. "I was bitter toward my husband, angry at God, and so afraid."

"Afraid?" Shay blinked in surprise.

"Terrified, actually." The small woman peered into the dusk. "I felt so alone and felt I had no control over anything. I prayed as hard as I have ever prayed."

"Did that help?" Shay backtracked. "I'm sorry. That's too personal a question. I guess I identify with you—I've prayed often for help, but sometimes it seems like God isn't listening."

"He is, my dear." Mrs. Green's fingers tightened around

hers. Perfect assurance filled her voice. "He hears every word you say. And yes, it did help me."

At that moment, Shay lifted her head and found Nick's gaze on her. He lifted one brow as if to ask if everything was okay. Shay nodded. He studied her for several moments before he went back to his storytelling.

"So, if God hears me, why doesn't He answer?" Shay asked the older woman.

"My dear girl, what makes you think He hasn't?"

Confused, Shay frowned.

"We must have a firm grip of knowledge about the love of God to fight our fears."

"I don't understand," Shay admitted, unsure where this was going.

"After I stopped ranting at God for allowing my husband to abandon me and our family, after I got past telling Him how He should fix my world, after my heart was completely empty and I couldn't fight anymore," Mrs. Green said as her eyes, so like her son's, met Shay's. "After I got past all of that, a wonderful thing happened. I began to listen."

Listen to what? Shay waited, needing to understand how this brave woman had conquered her fear and her anger.

"Perhaps I should say I began to hear." Mrs. Green smiled. "I remember the moment so clearly. I read a verse in Romans that said because of our faith Jesus brought us into this place of highest privilege where we now stand." Her laughter bubbled up into a chuckle. "You may believe me, my dear Shay, when I tell you I didn't think I was in any place of privilege, trying to feed and clothe five hungry kids on my own."

Shay smiled at her self-mocking tone, but she couldn't wait for the older woman to continue. Maybe here, at last, she'd find the solution to her panic.

"The next part of that verse says, 'We confidently and joyfully look forward to becoming all that God has in mind for us to be.' I was curious about that," Mrs. Green continued. "What could God have in mind for me, a single mom who didn't know where her next dollar was coming from? Was I going to be rescued, like Cinderella?"

Shay chuckled.

"I know." Mrs. Green shook her silvery head. "Me as Cinderella? Hardly. The next part says, 'We can rejoice when we run into problems and trials, for we know that they are good for us—they help us learn to be patient.'"

Shay nodded, familiar with the verse.

"I really, really *did not* want to learn patience just then, but what choice did I have? I repeated those words to myself day after day until I had them memorized."

Was there a way that Shay could put them into practice for herself? What would her life be like without the fear?

"'And patience...helps us trust God more each time we use it until finally our hope and faith are strong and steady.'" Mrs. Green beamed, her brown eyes shining with a joy that flowed from deep inside. "Isn't that wonderful? God so loves us that He teaches us to trust Him."

"But—" Shay started to argue.

"I realized that God always gave us enough. My children ate, they slept safely in their own home, they finished school." She touched Shay's shoulder, her fingers gentle. "I learned the truth of that passage. 'We are able to hold our heads high no matter what happens, and we know that all is well, for we know how dearly God loves us.'"

But God's love hadn't ended her panic attacks. Frustration nipped at Shay.

"You see, Shay, our part is to trust in Him and move on in our faith." Mrs. Green touched her cheek with a swollen knuckle. "The Bible promises, 'His peace will guard your hearts and minds as you live in Christ Jesus.'"

Silence stretched between them. Shay replayed the words

mentally. *His peace will guard your heart and mind.* Peace from her fears sounded so wonderful.

"Jaclyn gave me a verse about God not giving us fear but power. I've been reciting it over and over—"

"Honey, it's not the repeating so much as it is letting His words sink into your heart so that you believe them." The older woman searched her gaze. "Nick told me about the stalker, Shay. I hope you don't mind?"

"I don't mind. The thing is," Shay murmured, "I'm not sure if God abandoned me or if I've abandoned Him since then. I've tried to make it better, only it seems like God is doing nothing to help me. I feel like I don't matter to Him."

"You *do* matter, Shay. You are His beloved child and He cares for you." Mrs. Green leaned toward her and pinned her with that intense gaze. "I know you were terrorized. That opened the door to fear. I know exactly how it creeps up. I've felt its tentacles sink into me."

"So what do I do?"

"You have to listen to another voice." Mrs. Green leaned closer, her face somber. "Listen to the whisper that says, 'I am God. I am here and I am in control. I know the things I have planned for you, to prosper you and not to harm you.' That voice is stronger than anything you'll ever face. It can help you overcome your fear, if you'll only listen to it."

"Story time is over." Nick stood before them.

Shay hadn't even noticed him leave the fire. She looked around. Their marshmallows roasted, weary, drooping children looked ready to climb into their beds without complaint.

"I'm coming, son." Mrs. Green rose then bent to cup Shay's cheek in her palm. "Any time you want to talk, let me know."

She held out her arms and Shay went into them. She could at last see a flicker of light at the end of the tunnel. She wasn't sure how it all worked. Not yet. But she knew she wanted the

peace Mrs. Green had. She wanted to overcome defeat, to refuse to let the fear control her world any longer.

"Thank you," she whispered in the woman's ear. "Thank
you so much."

"Grandma, what are you and Shay whispering about?"
Maggie moved her Tiger machine with the big bicycle wheels
alongside her grandmother, yawning mightily as she did.

"I was just telling Shay about God and how much He loves
us," her grandmother explained.

"But Shay's big," Maggie said with a frown. "Doesn't she
already know that? I'm five and I know God loves me."

"How do you know, Maggie?" Shay asked.

Maggie leaned her head to one side to think about it. "Like
how I asked Him to please help me come to Grandma's party."
She shrugged. "I'm here, so that's how I know God loves me."

"Thank you for explaining that to me." Shay smiled at Nick
over Maggie's head as she hugged the sweet child.

"Time to get you home, darling." Her grandmother shared
a look with Maggie. Their faces glowed with the knowledge
that they were loved.

That, Shay realized, was what she longed for most of all.
To be loved.

The Green family took their leave, each one hugging Shay
and thanking her, until only Nick remained. He walked with
her to the house and switched off the lights they'd strung.

"Are you sure there's nothing more that needs doing?"
he asked.

"No. It's all finished. Everything is back to normal," Shay
said with a smile.

"Everything?" He tilted his head to one side, brushing a
strand of hair from her eyes.

She bit her lip and forced herself not to ease away from
Nick. "I know I lost it there in the garage. Thank you for coming to my rescue. Again."

"Listen. I've been thinking." He shuffled his feet in the gravel then lifted his head, his dark eyes hidden in the shadows. "This fear—it's tearing you apart. I thought maybe I could help. There's supposed to be a meteor shower in a couple of weeks—in the desert," he emphasized.

Dread of being alone in the desert's vast expanse surged. Shay opened her mouth to say no. Then she remembered Mrs. Green's words.

Face it. Trust God. Overcome.

"I promise you'll be safe, Shay. I'll—"

She reached up and with the briefest touch, laid a fingertip against his lips to stem his words. "I want to go," she said quietly.

Nick looked stunned by her acceptance. Or maybe it was that she'd touched him. When he finally snapped back to awareness, his dark eyes grew intense, his face earnest.

"Then we'll go. Together. I'll be right there, Shay."

"Thank you." Doubts about her decision swarmed. *What if, what if, what if...*

"I guess I'd better get going."

"Okay." She pressed her hands behind her, wishing he didn't have to leave, wishing he could stay and talk, help her chase away the panic that always came at night.

Wishing she could just be with him.

"Thank you for giving my mother this wonderful day, Shay." His gaze held hers. "We couldn't have done it without you."

"That's what friends are for." The way Nick stared at her made Shay's knees liquefy. Did he want to stay as much as she wanted him to?

"You went a long way past friendship today. So thank you."

Then Nick Green leaned forward and pressed a kiss against her cheek.

A moment later he was gone and Shay was left standing in

her yard, staring after him. She lifted one hand and touched the spot of tingling skin where his lips had landed for one brief second.

Now why had he gone and done that? she wondered as her heart skipped a few beats before it began to soar.

And if he was going to kiss me, why did it have to be on the cheek?

Shocked by the yearning that surged through her to be held in Nick's strong arms, Shay rushed into the house.

How come the prospect of such a thing filled her with joy and not fear?

Chapter Nine

"So Nick kissed you?" Brianna put her elbows on her desk and tucked her chin into her cupped palms. The gleam of interest in her eyes couldn't be disguised by the scholarly glasses she always wore for their sessions.

"Yes, he kissed me. On the cheek." Shay closed her eyes, still able to feel his lips. In fact, little else had been on her mind ever since it happened. Her brain kept replaying the scene over and over and her skin still tingled at the memory. That's why she'd made an appointment to talk to Brianna. Because she was so confused.

"And? What happened when Nick kissed you?"

"Nothing." Shay blinked at the realization.

"You didn't panic? You didn't freeze?" Brianna smiled at her surprise. "You trusted Nick enough to let him get that close."

"Or I was too stunned to react," Shay mumbled. Nothing seemed straightforward since Nick's kiss.

"You've never been that stunned before." Brianna smiled as she tented her fingers. "You've always managed to react before anyone else could get too close, including Eric."

"Nick surprised me, that's all. Don't you think?" Shay frowned.

"Is that what you want to believe?" Brianna asked.

"I don't know. Everything seems so mixed up." Shay rubbed her shoulder. "I can't make sense of myself."

"Because things are changing," Brianna suggested.

"Changing?" Shay couldn't make sense of what her friend meant. Or maybe she didn't want to? "You know, maybe this fear thing—maybe it's a personal flaw, something that can't be fixed."

"Why would you think that?"

"Because I look around and everyone else is happy. So I start to think, 'I can be happy, too. Today I'm not going to be afraid.'" Shay sighed as she slouched in her chair. "And then some stupid little thing happens and all I can think is— Dom's back."

"I wonder if that *is* what you think." Brianna fixed Shay with a serious stare.

"Huh?"

"Hear me out. I wonder if somewhere deep inside, when you're uncomfortable, your mind protests with fear because your subconscious is trying to protect you, to prevent a repeat of the out-of-control situation with the stalker."

"You think?" Shay rubbed her arms, desperate to get rid of the chills she was feeling.

"Tell me when you're most comfortable, Shay."

"When I'm at home, working on a project."

"Really? You're not getting up every five seconds to see if someone's out there?" She nodded at the look of surprise on Shay's face. "I thought so. Try again. When are you the *most* comfortable?" she prodded.

A second passed before Shay found the answer.

"Working with the kids."

"You're not afraid then?" her friend asked.

"Of course not." Shay blinked. "Why would I be? They're smaller than me—usually."

"I doubt that's the only reason." Brianna raised an eyebrow. "Can I tell you why I think you're totally comfortable with yourself when you're with the kids?"

"You're the shrink." Shay wondered if she was going to like hearing this.

"Technically, I'm a psychologist, but moving on." Brianna leaned forward. "You're completely relaxed when you're with kids because your focus is off you. You're thinking about how you can help them."

"Okay. So?" Shay didn't get it.

"Your panic stems from when you start thinking about what might happen. You're letting 'might' dictate how you live your life, Shay."

"I'm not that bad." Shay bristled at the intimation. "I have a...normal life."

"Really?" A tiny smile played at the corner of Brianna's lips. "You're a young, beautiful woman. You broke up with Eric, what, eight, ten months ago? Have you had a date since then?"

"No, but Eric was a doctor. He understood my situation."

"And yet, he broke up with you." Brianna's implacable expression told Shay she had to face facts.

"Right. But—" Shay bit her lip. "It doesn't matter anyway because I don't think God wants me to be in a romantic relationship."

"God doesn't? Or you don't, because you don't want to get hurt again?" Brianna stood, moved around her desk and sank down next to Shay. "Tell me—what would happiness look like to you?"

"Living on my farm with a family," Shay replied with a promptness that surprised her. "Helping kids during the day, sharing life with someone."

"A family." Brianna paused to let that sink in. "In that world you're safe because you've got everything under control. Only you don't, do you? Because life isn't like that. It's messy and things happen when you least expect them. Like Nick kissing you." She smiled. "You can't preprogram your life because you're afraid, darlin'. And you have to stop expecting you can revert back to the woman you were before the stalker."

"Then what do I do?" Shay demanded, frustrated.

"Stop trying to keep yourself safe." Brianna shook her head when Shay tried to interrupt. "Face your fears, sweetie. It's time."

"You're saying I should go with Nick and watch the meteor shower?" Heat scorched her cheeks at the thought of it. "What if he...kisses me again?"

"Would that be so terrible?" Brianna asked.

"What if he kisses me and I end up in the middle of the desert, cowering under a cactus? What then?"

"Who better than your responsible best friend, Nick Green, to make sure you get home safely?" Brianna asked. "*Let go,* Shay. Trust Nick. He might surprise you. You might surprise yourself." She wrapped an arm around her shoulder. "Just remember, you're not alone. And you're certainly not helpless."

"What do you mean?"

"You have God on your side." Brianna grinned. "If God be for us..." she said, reciting the mantra she, Jaclyn and Shay had often used back in high school.

"...who can be against us?" Shay finished.

Who indeed?

Nick sat in Shay's yard, reliving the memory of the kiss he'd planted on her after his mom's party. Two weeks later and the joy he'd felt that night wasn't any easier to suppress. But it seemed as if he was alone in that reaction because when Shay started showing up several evenings a week for Bible study with his mom, she pretended nothing had changed between them.

Maybe for her, nothing *had* changed.

But for Nick, things were definitely different. First of all, he couldn't stop wondering what might have happened if Shay had turned her head and let him kiss her lips. He was pretty sure there would have been fireworks.

What was new was that Nick had finally accepted that he wanted more than that little peck on the cheek from Shay—and knew he couldn't have it. God's plans included him leaving Hope, so despite his over-the-top reaction, there was no way he and Shay could be anything more than friends.

And he wanted to be her friend. But he also wanted more...

Nick forced himself off that subject to think about whether he'd included everything they'd need for this evening in the desert, and then spent a few minutes praying for guidance. He was no longer certain this trip was the right thing for Shay. After all, what did he really know about anxiety attacks? How could he possibly understand what she was going through?

And yet, in a way, he did know. Nick got that same throat-clenching worry every time he thought about that job in Seattle. What if his family needed him and he wasn't there for them? His stomach dipped when he imagined Maggie and his mom on their own, maybe needing his help but too proud or too embarrassed to let him know.

Every day Nick watched the two of them and knew the situation couldn't last forever. Though she loved her granddaughter dearly, his mom was overtaxing herself. Maggie was a little kid. She wanted to run and jump and yell, as all kids did. Even with him here to help, his mom tired easily. She needed time for herself. When Maggie went to school, that would help. But...

The what-ifs tortured him.

And what about Shay? Who would be here to help her?

Who else knew exactly how deeply the stalker had affected her life?

Nick had no answers to any of those questions.

"Hi." Shay's quiet voice jerked Nick out of his introspection.

"Hi, yourself."

"Any particular reason you've been sitting out here for the past ten minutes?" She waited, her head tipped to one side in a quizzical look.

"Not really." He climbed out of the truck. "Shay, I'm not sure about this—"

"I am, Nick." She lifted her shoulders and looked him straight in the eye. "Your mom told me how her faith changed after your dad left. As we've studied together, she's shown me how childish I've been about my panic. Even Maggie's faith is bigger than mine." Her wide, generous mouth tipped down at the corners as if she was fighting back tears. A moment later Shay was back in control. "But that is going to change. Starting tonight."

"Oh?" Nick couldn't imagine what his mother had said to ignite the light of battle in Shay, but he was glad to see it. The very thought of brave, strong Shay huddled up on her car hood pierced an arrow right through his heart every time.

"I've been letting my fear cast out God's love. No more. I'm trusting God now."

"Good." He smiled at the flash of fire in those emerald eyes.

She threw her jacket over one shoulder and arched an eyebrow at him. "You have my permission to remind me of those words. Now, are you ready to go?"

"Sure." Nick grabbed his knapsack from the truck and slipped the straps over his shoulders. "Let's go see what movie God's playing on the big screen tonight." He slung two folding chairs over his shoulder then held out his hand.

Shay hesitated just long enough that he started to drop his hand. Then she stretched out her arm and threaded her fingers into his. Her laugh had a wobble in it, but her grin was all Shay-of-the-old-days.

"I'm thinking it's going to be a double feature," she joked.

"I even brought popcorn." His pulse skipped at the touch of her soft skin against his palm.

She's a friend. That's all. Remember?

They weren't far into their walk when Shay withdrew her hand, ostensibly to brush a strand of hair from her face. Nick was pretty sure she'd done it to put distance between them. But that was okay—she'd managed to keep hold of his hand for a few minutes. It was a start.

Part of him mourned that he wouldn't be around to see her triumph, but he was going to make every moment he did have with her count.

"Nick?" Shay touched his arm to stop him.

"Yeah?" He glanced around, searching for something that might have startled her. He saw nothing.

Shay said in a perfectly normal tone of voice, "I've been trying to figure out how you made those bicycle wheels on Maggie's Tiger work."

"Top secret," he said, crossing his fingers and placing them against his heart as if he'd made some kind of promise.

"You know I hate secrets. Tell me." Shay gave him a fake glare.

"Uh-uh." The urge to tease grew. "If I told you, I'd have to—"

Kiss you? Stunned by how much he wanted to, Nick gulped and struggled to regroup.

"You'd have to what, Nick?" she prodded, waiting for him to finish.

Now was so not the time. But later he was going to have

a strict talk with himself about a certain lady named Shay. Nick grabbed her hand and tugged.

"We have to talk as we walk or we'll miss the show."

She drew her hand out of his after only a few steps and rapped his shoulder in reproof.

"Seriously, how'd you figure it out?" she demanded as she returned her fingers to the cradle of his.

Nick looked at her and his stomach knot tightened. That had been happening a lot lately—like whenever he was around Shay. When Shay was near, Nick saw pure possibilities. Which was stupid, because there was no future possibility for them, he reminded himself.

"I stopped by the seniors' hall to pick up something for Mom," he explained. "They were working on an old Model T, so I pitched in." He drew her near as they sidestepped some low-hanging mesquite trees. "While we were working, one of the guys mentioned he was struggling to adapt his current project. I fiddled with it and figured it out, and it gave me the idea for Maggie's wheels."

"Well, that was good." Shay inhaled deeply.

Nick noticed her eyes dart from side to side for a moment. He kept talking, hoping to distract her.

"Maybe not. I got talked into meeting with them after their coffee hour on Saturday mornings." Nick rolled his eyes. "They think I'm some kind of superrepairman. They're going to bring stuff from home so I can show them how to fix it."

"How can that be bad?" Shay's forehead creased in a frown.

"Shay, I tear stuff apart. I don't put it back together."

"So now you will." She laughed at the face he made.

"Unlikely. But they won't take no for an answer, so I'll do my best to help."

"Like you helped Mrs. Campbell get her thirty-year-old

dishwasher working?" she asked, her lips curling in a coy smile.

"Exactly. Look how that turned out. I nearly flooded her house in the process." He stepped around a teddy bear cactus. "I was trying to do her a favor, to thank her for giving us that old bicycle."

"A favor, huh?" Shay nodded, her face solemn. "The same kind of favor you did Susan Swan and her sink? And of course, you couldn't walk away without fixing some kind of weight machine so Susan's husband could exercise his arm, could you?" she said, tongue in cheek.

"Don't make me out to be some kind of hero, Shay. I just like to tinker." Nick grabbed her arm when she misstepped on a rocky area. "Careful. Stick close."

"As close as a tick." Her fingers tightened around his. He couldn't deny how he loved the feel of her hand in his. It was almost more than he could stand. "I could continue to list things you've done around town to help people, Nick," she went on. "Seems like everyone has a story about you." She chewed on her bottom lip for a moment before she blurted out, "I think you should advertise. You could start up a business."

"A business?" Nick frowned at her.

"Don't look at me like that. It's a good idea."

"Doing what? I don't have any training or certification. Who would pay me to tinker with their stuff?" He appreciated the thought, but it had taken him four hours to figure out he needed a two-dollar seal to get that wreck of a dishwasher working. No one would pay him by the hour to learn on the job, and Nick needed the assurance of a steady income.

They walked a little farther in silence, each lost in their thoughts. Then Shay's small hand started to squeeze his.

"How much farther?" she whispered. He knew she was fighting back her panic at the blackness surrounding them.

"Just up that rise." Nick pointed and heard her breath catch as she recognized where they were. She inhaled in short gasps as they climbed the steep hill.

"This is where Dad taught me about astronomy." Her voice wasn't exactly calm—more like determined. But it wasn't full of panic, and that made Nick happier than he could have imagined. "I used to love coming up here."

"I remember. Look."

Ahead of them stars twinkled and glittered like diamonds tossed onto black velvet. Nick kept his grip on Shay's hand, just to make sure that she was okay, that she knew he was there if she needed him.

At least, that's what he told himself.

In truth, standing here with her, sharing this moment, made his own breathing uneven. Beautiful Shay, so near he wanted to draw her into the protection of his arms and kiss her. But that would betray her trust.

Nothing more than friendship, he reminded himself.

Beside him, Shay gasped. "Our heavenly star show is starting. See that?" She pointed upward, tracking a meteor as it flew across the sky. "And that?"

"I see it." Nick fell silent, awestruck by the glorious shower of lights.

"It's like God is lighting them especially for us." Shay's eyes blazed with excitement. "Look how they sparkle and blaze and then fizzle away, their tails glowing. Beautiful."

Shay's words chided him, reminding him that his faith wasn't as strong as it should be. It wasn't only Shay who needed to stop trying to be in control.

Her breath tickled his neck when she turned her head. "Fearfully and wonderfully made," she whispered.

Yes, she was. But he had a hunch Shay wasn't talking about herself. "I've heard that before somewhere," Nick said.

"It's a verse your mom quoted." Shay turned her head to smile at him. "The Bible says we are fearfully and wonderfully made by God. Everything in the universe has a purpose, a reason, a private beauty."

Moonbeams cast Shay's hair in a golden sheen. Nick's gaze tangled with hers, and for a moment neither of them said anything. Just as Nick was wondering how to fight off the urge to kiss her again, a noise startled Shay. Her green eyes widened as she asked in a shaky tone, "What was that?"

"I've got you, Shay. "Nick slid an arm around her waist and hugged her against his side. "Nothing bad is going to happen. And God's on duty, too. Relax and enjoy His show."

It took a few moments before she relaxed enough to lean against him. When she turned her head to study him, a tiny smile pulled up the corners of her lush lips.

"You're my very best friend, Nick." She tilted her head to rest it on his shoulder for a brief moment before she stepped away and hugged her waist. "Thank you."

"For what?" he asked. He had a hunch Shay was about to say something important, something she didn't tell just anyone.

"For being you. For not caring that I'm scared all the time. A coward." She didn't look at him as she continued speaking, her voice dropping to a near-whisper. "I think it's only here, tonight, with you, that I realize how great a gift you are. Eric claimed to love me, but he was never as patient with my fears as you have been."

"Eric?" Nick went cold inside at that name. His stomach tightened and his heart skipped a beat. It took a moment to define what he was feeling. Jealous—he was jealous of Shay's former boyfriend.

"We were a couple." Her husky laugh made a mockery of mirth. She seemed oblivious to the burst of emotions exploding inside him. "He said he loved me. I thought I loved him, too. But whenever he touched me, I'd freeze up."

"He didn't force—" Nick couldn't say it.

"Oh, no. Eric was kindness itself. He tried hard to understand what I was going through. For months he tried. But he wanted a wife. He needed someone who could respond to his love."

The shame in those words lit an angry fire inside Nick. "You couldn't have been that bad."

"I was." In the flare of a meteor, her green eyes looked wounded by the admission. "We would be having fun and then he'd put his arm around my shoulder or hug me and it was like being choked. I couldn't breathe. But I couldn't tell him what was wrong, either."

Nick didn't give a fig about Eric but he hated that Shay looked so decimated, that she felt she was to blame for the breakdown of the relationship.

"I'm sorry," he murmured, feeling utterly helpless.

"Your mom says I didn't trust Eric." She stopped abruptly and tilted her head to one side. "She's right. I find it hard to trust anyone after…"

"The stalker." Everything always came back to that. "But why? That guy was never someone you trusted. Was he?"

"I didn't even know him!" Shay turned and stared at him. "Why did you ask that?"

"I guess because you blame your lack of trust on the stalker."

"And?" Those world-famous lips pressed into a straight line.

Nick had never been good with words or emotions. But he was going to say this because he'd thought about Shay's problems a lot and he figured maybe he was on to something. "Everything started after your dad died, right?"

Shay nodded but said nothing. As she listened, her focus returned to the dance of meteors above them.

"Well." Nick watched the flash and dazzle of the light show

as he spoke from his heart. "I wonder if you felt abandoned by his loss and that made you more…susceptible."

"You're saying it's all a trick I'm deliberately playing on myself?" Anger threaded through Shay's voice and she turned on him. "You think I get myself up in the middle of the night to check outside because I'm nuts?"

"That isn't what I'm saying." Nick unfolded one of the chairs and held it for her. "Sit down and let's talk about this. We're alone here. You can say whatever you want. Nothing you tell me will shock me."

She thought about it for a while.

"You said you were going to face your fear," he reminded.

"I did, didn't I?" Shay flopped into the chair, slouched and thrust her long legs out in front of her. "But if I'm crazy, so are you."

"I'm willing to explore the possibility," he said as he unfolded his own chair and sat down beside her. "Exactly why am I crazy?"

"Because your family—the most precious thing in the world—is right here in Hope, and you're bound and determined to leave them and go off someplace where you won't be able to see them." She crossed her arms as if daring him to deny it, her gaze on the sky. "That's about the craziest thing ever."

"I have to work," Nick told her flatly.

"Why can't you work here?" She turned her head, her hair swishing around her face. "There are lots of things you could do, lots of people you could help in Hope."

"I have to earn a living, Shay." Nick ignored her irritated glance. "I can't do that in Hope."

She'd turned the tables, focusing the conversation on him. But before he could explain again why he needed to go back to Seattle, Shay's eyes filled with unshed tears.

"Lately it seems everyone's telling me I have trust issues.

You just did, too," she reminded, her voice tight. "But everyone has them."

"Of course they do. Trust is one of the hardest things to give."

"That's why you're determined to leave here," she said so quietly he almost didn't hear. "You don't trust God."

Nick was stunned by her comment. Suddenly, one meteor blazed brighter than all the rest and set off the desert in stark relief before it winked out, plunging them into darkness again.

"All that caring you have inside you will fizzle out, just like the meteorites, because you don't trust God or me or your mom," Shay continued. "You don't even trust Maggie."

Nick opened his mouth to reply, but he couldn't tell her that for years he'd trusted God to bring his dad back, or about how he'd been bitterly disappointed. He couldn't tell her why it was so hard to keep trusting.

"I think you're the most admirable man I've ever known, next to my dad. You care for everyone. You've done your best to do that from the day your dad left." Shay's green eyes met his. "But Nick, you can't make up for what your dad did."

"Yes, Shay, I can. And I am."

But Shay shook her head. "You can't because it isn't your mistake to make up for." She touched his arm, her sweet face intent. "Your mother loves you, Nick, and she loves everything you do for her and the rest of the family. But you can't erase the hurt your father caused her. You shouldn't even try."

"I have to," he said, his jaw clenched. "She's a wonderful person. It's not fair that she should—"

"When did we get a promise of fairness in this life?" Shay's smile eased the sting of her words. "I know I have problems, Nick. But don't spend all your time trying to help me. Help yourself, too."

"I don't know what you mean." He couldn't look at her.

"I mean that you don't have to prove that you're not your

dad. I doubt there's a single soul in town who thinks you'd abandon those who count on you." Shay cupped his cheek in her palm. "The only one who doesn't seem to believe in you is you."

She was right, and he knew it.

"The job in Seattle—you don't really want to take it, do you, Nick?" The intensity of Shay's gaze and the wistfulness of her words prevented him from lying.

"No." A wave of relief washed over him as he finally admitted the truth. "It's not the work," he assured her as another blaze exploded above them. "I could enjoy helping the guys reach their potential. It's just that with Georgia gone—" Why did it still hurt so much?

"You're worried about your mom and Maggie," she finished, her fingers squeezing his.

"My mother puts up a good front, but being responsible for Maggie is wearing her out."

"So stay here in Hope."

"Shay, we've been through this." Frustrated, Nick raked his hand through his hair. "How can I stay in Hope and still support my family?"

"I don't know, Nick. I don't have all the answers. But I know who does. Why don't you try asking Him what His will for you is?"

A wry smile lifted his lips. How could he tell her he didn't have enough faith to do that? How could he admit that he'd been so deeply disappointed by the loss of his career, so shattered by Georgia's death, so angry God hadn't answered his prayer about his father that he now was afraid of God, afraid He'd dole out another sucker punch and that it would completely destroy the threadbare remnants of faith Nick now clung to? Nick was so scared of what God would do that he was afraid to even consider that the growing feelings he had for Shay could ever be realized.

"You're just like me, Nick." Shay's whisper was all the more emphatic in the silence of the evening. "Neither of us trusts God enough. And we must. It's time you and I began trusting God with our futures."

As they sat silently together in the darkness of the desert, watching heaven unfold its mysteries, lost in their own thoughts, Nick glanced at Shay. Her attention was riveted on the flashing spectacle above. Her lips moved in what he thought was a prayer.

Nick claimed he was a Christian. He professed to believe in God's love. Maybe Shay was right. Maybe it was time to prove it.

Moments, maybe hours later—he wasn't sure how much time had passed—the last flash blinked into nothingness and the world finally returned to normal. Shay rose. Her face glowed with radiance only a transformational inner experience could have given.

She said nothing as they walked back to her house, and Nick was content with that. But he was surprised when she wrapped her fingers around his as he walked her to her front porch.

"Would you like to come inside?" she murmured.

That surprised him even more. Shay looked and sounded different. Not exactly serene, but not filled with the panic he'd glimpsed earlier. Clearly the meteor shower and their talk had affected her. He wanted desperately to go inside, to talk some more, to be near her.

To stay.

But what he wanted wasn't possible.

"It's late. I'd better get home."

"Okay." Her lovely smile flashed white in the gloom as she stared at him. "I want to thank you for such a wonderful evening, Nick. Now, whenever I go into the desert, I'm going to think of this meteor shower and remember that God's love is like a cloak of meteors showering down all around me, protecting me."

He debated about the best way to say what was on his mind but in the end decided it would be wrong to keep this from her any longer. Besides, something about the change in her tonight made him believe that she could deal with what he had to say, and he so wanted her to be able to get rid of the past.

"Shay?"

"Yes?" Her innocent green eyes held his.

"I've been in contact with the New York Police Department."

"Wha—why?" she stammered. He could almost feel her anxiety building like static in the air around them.

"I wanted to know if they'd ever caught your stalker." He waited but she said nothing. "They haven't." Her reaction, the way she seemed to freeze up, told him he should have waited. But he couldn't stop now. Nick struggled to find the best way to say it, but there was no way to put a good spin on this. "For over a year they've been chasing a guy who's stalking other women."

"I'm sorry." Her face froze into an ivory mask.

"The thing is, Shay, he has almost the same M.O. as your stalker. If it is the same guy, he's become much more adept at hiding his identity. His victims are terrified."

Her posture grew increasingly rigid until finally she burst out, "What do you want from me, Nick?"

"I was hoping you'd agree to talk to the police, review your experience to see if there are any clues that could stop this creep and save other women the harm you've suffered." His heart ached for the rush of emotions that cracked her mask of calm.

Shay seemed frozen to the spot. Though not a muscle moved, he knew her panic battled for control. Then she lifted her head and looked straight at him. Her lips lifted in a mirth-less smile.

"So it's time to put my money where my mouth is," she said. "Time to prove that I will trust God."

"Shay, I didn't mean—" One look from those green eyes silenced him.

Her shoulders went back, her spine straightened and her chin thrust out.

"Okay," she said. "I'll talk to the police in the morning." She seemed somehow frailer, somehow diminished, but her tone was resolute. "I will not be a coward anymore."

"You could never be a coward."

Nick couldn't help himself—he drew her into his arms, pressed her head to his shoulder and breathed in the soft lemon scent of her hair. "You're the strongest, most amazing, most caring and most compassionate woman I know." He cupped her face in his palms and drew back to look into her eyes. "I'll be with you, Shay. I'll be right by your side. We'll do it together."

"Together." A spark of gold flared in her green eyes. "Can you arrange a conference call for eight a.m. tomorrow?"

He nodded.

"Okay then." She exhaled then eased away. "You really know how to show a girl a good time, Nick."

The right words wouldn't come to him, the words he needed to tell her how much he admired her, how she was the most special woman he'd ever met. So Nick did the only thing he could think of. He drew her close and kissed her on the lips, pouring the kaleidoscope of his feelings into that embrace.

When he released her, Shay's glazed look made him want to do it again. But he couldn't.

Nick said good-night and strode to his truck.

Shay said his mom had taught her about trusting God.

Maybe it was time he sought some parental advice for himself. Nick knew nothing would change between him and Shay— no matter how much he wanted things to be different, he was still responsible for his family.

But maybe he could do something about the gulf between him and God.

Chapter Ten

"So you've got *another* machine? How many is that now?"

"I don't know." Maggie frowned as she pushed her foot against Shay's hand. "There's my roly-poly, my Tiger and the giggle machine."

"The giggle machine? What is that?" Shay glanced at Nick standing nearby in the physical therapy room and blushed, remembering his kiss after the meteor show. It had been two weeks and she still couldn't stop thinking about that kiss, or the way he'd held her hand through every conference call they'd had with the NYPD.

"Uncle Nick calls it a giggle machine because it makes me laugh when I use it." Maggie puffed with exertion.

"Think of a weird version of a treadmill," Nick said to Shay. His brown eyes twinkled when she lifted one eyebrow. "Really weird."

"It is weird," Maggie agreed, brown eyes widening. "Because sometimes when I walk on it, nothing happens. And then all of a sudden, something does. Once a balloon blew up right in front of me!"

Shay smiled as she urged Maggie to push a little harder.

"If you came to Grandma's, I could show you," Maggie hinted.

Shay had deliberately stayed away from the Green home because of Nick. Or, more accurately, because of his kiss. It set odd feelings alight inside her, and that made her nervous. She was coming to rely on him too much. So she'd buried herself in helping Jaclyn with restorations on their old church. And slowly, solace began to replace fear as Scripture seeped into her heart.

The hours of discussion with the police tested Shay's baby steps of faith, leaving her feeling wobbly, her fragile sense of security shaken. Reliving the terror of those days when she'd been so vulnerable to her stalker had challenged her determination to trust God. Some days it felt as if she was hanging on by a mere thread, but Shay *did* hang on, refusing to give in to the fear.

Nick, with his unswerving comfort and support, had now become such an integral part of her world that Shay wasn't sure how she would fare when he left. But she was only too aware that her time with him was running out. And then she'd be alone.

Again.

But that's the way it had to be because she couldn't love or be loved…until she'd defeated the panic for good.

I can do all things through Christ who strengthens me. I can do all things through Christ who strengthens me…

"Shay?" Maggie touched her arm. "When will you come to see my giggle machine?"

"I'll stop by as soon as I can," Shay promised before leading Maggie through the rest of her exercises. "You're doing much better," she said, surprised by the child's progress in the past week. "Uncle Nick's machines are really helping you, huh?"

"Or maybe it's her excellent therapist," Nick chimed in from the end of the bars.

"Well, naturally that's a given," she joked. "But if you

polled the folks in Hope, I'm guessing Nick Green would be the one they'd nominate as most valuable citizen." She tossed him a grin. "There doesn't seem to be anyone who doesn't think you deserve the town's top award, maybe even a crown."

"It's a distinct possibility Heddy Grange might crown me with something, but I doubt it would be gold or jewels," Nick said in a droll tone. "I didn't exactly fix that fountain of hers. In fact, she said I broke it."

Shay looked at Maggie. They tried to keep straight faces but a second later they burst into laughter.

"When she plugged it in," Maggie spluttered, "the water came out of the swan's mouth and hit Uncle Nick in the face!"

"Go ahead and laugh," Nick said, his pique evident in the spots of bright red dotting his cheekbones. "I told you, Shay, I am not a handyman. But I could easily come up with a list of things I'd like to do with that swan." His gorgeous eyes glinted. "And most of them involve a hammer."

His malevolent glare only made Shay laugh harder. She caught Maggie's eye and winked.

"At least your debacle didn't make it into the paper," she said. "Heddy loves to get her name on the front page, you know."

The words had no sooner left her lips than an idea dawned. "Maggie, what would you think about showing off what you and the others have achieved these past months? You can invite your grandma and anyone else you'd like. Uncle Nick can come, too."

"Like a demonstration?" Maggie breathed with shining eyes. "Ted, too?"

"Yep, for all of my kids. Saturday afternoon. I want you to bring your giggle machine and your Tiger machine, Maggie. Nick, you bring that new gizmo you've been working on for the seniors' fitness class you started."

Shay thought if she could show Nick the difference he and

his machines had made in people's lives, if he realized that he was needed here—maybe then he'd reconsider staying. Shay wanted Nick to be happy. Wouldn't he be happier in Hope, with his mother and Maggie, than in Seattle?

Of course she wanted Nick to stay for her, too. Shay wanted him to stay because she was sure he was as affected by that kiss as she was, because she wanted to spend more time with him, because…

Wait! This is about Nick's happiness. Not my…feelings.

Shay made a mental note to phone the newspaper to suggest a human-interest story. The whole town was talking about Nick—surely it wouldn't be hard to steer a reporter toward a profile of Nick's work. And once her buddy recognized the difference he made here in Hope, he'd change his mind about leaving.

"So, uh, anything else?" Nick asked.

"Oh, sorry." She helped Maggie put her braces back on. "Pretty soon you won't need these," she whispered in the child's ear.

"Really?" The brown eyes expanded. "When can I walk all by myself?"

"If you keep working hard, pretty soon." Shay's heart warmed at Maggie's whoop of joy.

"I am going to beat Ted," she said, a fierce determination filling her face.

"Don't think about that," Nick said, scooping her into his arms. His gaze rested on Shay, as if he were trying to transmit a secret message. "Forget everyone and everything. Keep your eye on the goal."

That was good advice—for Maggie and for her.

Because at this moment, the goal was to get Nick to see that he was needed here. Shay couldn't imagine life in Hope without Nick.

Actually, she couldn't imagine *life* without Nick. Period.

* * *

"So what's your role in this?" Ben Marks demanded as he snapped several shots of Shay's kids.

"Me? I'm just the fix-it guy. And a cheerleader." Nick deliberately downplayed his contribution to the local reporter because he wanted all the focus to be on Shay and the wonderful things she'd done for these children. Fierce pride filled him as he watched her instill confidence in each of her clients. "She's a miracle worker, that's for sure."

The reporter moved in for another shot and Nick headed for his seat. Maggie was onstage next and he didn't want to miss a second. As he sat down beside his mom, he heard her gasp and glanced up. What he saw made his own heart skip a beat.

Maggie stepped free of her braces and walked three steps in a halting, jerky gait.

But she *walked*.

A lump the size of Gibraltar lodged in Nick's throat. He couldn't say anything. He could only stare as his niece, triumphant, stood grinning as Shay put her braces back on.

When her last clients finished their display, Shay introduced each one again, beaming with joy and satisfaction. The kids took a final bow then hurried over to their loved ones, eager to crow about their achievements. Maggie was no different and moved quickly toward them with her Tiger machine.

"I beat Ted!" she blurted, her joy boundless.

"So that's what you and Shay have been doing the past few days." Nick hugged her tightly, thanking God for the gift of healing He'd given this precious child. "That's quite a secret you've been keeping, Maggie-mine. I'm surprised you didn't burst with it."

His mother, tears flowing down her cheeks, couldn't say anything. All she could do was wrap her granddaughter in a hug until finally Maggie squealed.

"Too tight, Grandma," Maggie protested and eased herself

free. "Shay's got doughnuts and cookies with pictures on them and fruit punch!" She waved at Ted and rushed toward him.

"I give thanks every day for that woman," his mother murmured as she dabbed at her eyes. "Shay Parker is a walking, talking blessing."

Yes, she is. Nick stood in the background, as proud as any parent, watching as Shay spoke with the families of her clients. How Nick wished he could stay in Hope and watch her break free of the fear that had kept her imprisoned for so long.

How he wished he could help her finish that part of her journey.

Shay posed for pictures with her kids. When Ben would have moved on, she asked him to take some with Nick and his inventions.

"He's a big part of the reason these kids have made such astounding progress," she bragged.

"This is your moment, Shay," Nick protested to no avail.

"It's a moment that wouldn't have happened at all without you, Nick. His work is amazing," she said to the photographer. "He has a gift for seeing what the kids need and creating exactly what will help them achieve their goals."

Nick's cell phone buzzed to let him know he had a text. He took out his phone as Shay and the photographer began setting up the shot. NYPD was trying to reach Shay, who had apparently turned off her phone. So they'd called him.

Why today? Nick could hardly bear the thought of extinguishing her joy, but it probably had to do with the stalker, and if it did he would be there for Shay.

He couldn't do anything about his burgeoning feelings for her. But he *could* stick by her side and be a true friend, regardless of the fact that his heart wanted more.

Nick got through the photos and waited until the last person had left to tell her. As he worked beside Shay to restore the room to its rightful appearance, he said, "Shay?"

"Yes?" She led him out of the room then locked the door. When he didn't immediately speak, she frowned. A guarded look filled her eyes—he hated being the cause of it. "What's wrong?"

"New York texted me," he told her quietly. "Our guy has been active again. They'd like to review what you told them and see if they can find something new."

She didn't protest, didn't argue that she'd told them all she knew. Shay Parker wasn't that kind of woman. Instead she inhaled, pushed back her shoulders and nodded. But the clouds in her eyes told him she was battling hard to retain her calm. "I'll go call them now." She turned.

"Shay?" Nick waited for her to look at him. "I'll stay. If you want me to."

"Yes," she said very quietly. "I do want you—to be there."

He caught the slight hesitation, but there was no time to think about that. He followed her into her office and while she dialed, he pushed a chair next to hers. When the questions began, he grasped her hand in his and held on all through the heart-wrenching process of reliving the worst days of her life—again.

And that's when Nick realized that leaving Hope and this amazing woman was going to be the hardest thing he ever did.

But he couldn't ignore the only opportunity God had given him to care for his family.

Could he?

Three hours later, all joy in her afternoon's achievement had drained away, leaving Shay tired and defeated. Nick hated that.

"I doubt they'll catch him," she said as she hung up the phone. "I couldn't give them enough. I don't *know* enough." She ran a hand through her copper curls, rubbing her scalp to ease her tension. "Or if I do, I can't remember."

"You did the best you could."

"It wasn't enough. They know it and so do I. I should have tried harder to figure it out back when I was going through it. I shouldn't have been so afraid."

"Anyone would have been afraid, Shay. Anyone would struggle as you have if they'd gone through what you did. Don't beat yourself up with what-ifs."

"I'll try not to." She summoned a tired smile. "Thank you for staying with me. I appreciate it."

"That's what friends are for." Which was true, except that Nick felt guilty for saying it because he knew he wanted to be a whole lot more than just Shay's friend. He returned his chair to its rightful place facing her desk then followed her to the front office. He paused by the door. "What now?"

"I'm going home to take a nice long bubble bath. Maybe that will ease this crick in my neck." As Shay locked the door she exhaled a puff of air that rustled the damp strands of hair on her forehead. "It's so hot today. I'm glad I left Hugs inside with the air on."

She would go home defeated and probably spend the night dreaming about the creep and the terror he was causing someone else. Nick couldn't allow that.

"I can trump the bubble bath," he said as he waited for her to unlock the car.

"Right this minute a bubble bath sounds like heaven to me," she said. "What have you got in mind?"

"A swim. At the lake."

"The lake, huh?" Her green eyes flickered with interest.

"Think about it." Nick figured he'd have to sell this if he wanted to spend more time with Shay this evening—which obviously, against his better judgment, he did. "Cool, refreshing water lapping over you. A soft breeze floating through the pines. You can swim, relax and work out the kinks. Hugs could run around—" Nick blinked. The wimpy name had slipped out without him even thinking about it. Because that was Shay's name for her dog. Because she'd chosen it with love.

Man, he cared a lot for this woman.

"Mmm. Perfect." Shay closed her eyes and stretched. "You're right, the lake will be far better than a bubble bath. When would we go?"

"I'll pick you up in half an hour." He hesitated, wishing he could spend the evening alone with her but knowing that his mom desperately needed some free time. "Do you mind if I bring Mags? Mom could probably use the break."

"Of course I don't mind. Swimming will be good for Maggie." She nodded. "I'll put a picnic together. We could roast some hot dogs if you build a fire."

"Now you're getting the picture." Nick paused, unsure of the words that would tell her how deeply affected he was by what she'd done today. "I can't thank you enough, Shay. Seeing Maggie walk those few steps this afternoon—it was incredible."

"No thanks needed. It's my job." She grinned, her green eyes sparkling. "I love that kid. And her faith is incredible. Georgia would be so proud of her."

"Yeah." He swallowed hard.

"Yeah." Shay touched his arm then got into her car. She cranked it a couple of times before the engine caught.

"You should get that checked," he told her.

"I've had it in the shop several times but they never find the problem. I guess I'll have to take it in again." She revved the motor. "See you in half an hour," she called before driving away.

"Yes, you will," he promised. As he drove home, Nick caught himself whistling the melody to a hymn and realized belatedly that it was "Only Believe," a song he hadn't heard since he was a kid. "All things are possible," the lyrics claimed. "Only believe."

All things?

Nick wasn't sure he understood that. This morning he'd received an email from his football squad wanting to know if he could start work a month early. The bonus the organization was offering was substantial enough to make him seriously consider it, despite his overwhelming reluctance to leave Hope and his family—and Shay.

Maggie was doing so much better now. Daily she grew more independent. As for his mom, well, Nick had talked to Heddy Grange about finding people to help with Maggie after he'd gone. That eased Nick's mind. His team's offering of a bonus would solve another worry; that cash would make a nice dent in the purchase price of a new minivan for his mom so she could retire her problem-plagued vehicle.

But no matter how he spun the benefits of that offer, Nick couldn't find a positive in leaving Shay. Talking to her, sharing their problems, finding ways to surmount them—that part of his life had become more important to him than he'd ever imagined it would.

Because Shay Parker was more than his friend.

Nick sat in his mother's yard and let the knowledge seep into his soul. He admired Shay's giving heart and the way she refused to back down. He treasured the way her enthusiastic laugh bubbled up from deep inside and spilled onto everyone around her. He adored the way she included all people and didn't care about opinions. How could he feel anything but the deepest respect and affection for a woman so generous she had to help every child she encountered?

But even if Nick did believe he could have a relationship with Shay, he wouldn't dream of asking her to leave her new life and the joy she'd found in Hope. And he couldn't stay here without a job.

For a moment he let himself dream of Shay with him in Seattle, riding up the Space Needle for dinner, cheering for his team, walking through the fine spring rain.

All things are possible? Not this time.

"This is one of those memory-making nights," Shay murmured, staring into the dying embers of the campfire. "In fifty years, I'll lie in my bed and still remember how bright the stars shone, how sweetly the birds sang, how fresh the air felt on my skin. Mostly I'll remember how alive I feel." She turned her head toward Nick. "Thank you for you suggesting this."

"I'm enjoying it, too," he said. *Enjoy* seemed such a tame word. He'd never laughed as hard as he had watching Shay and Maggie revel in the buoyancy of the water as they turned somersaults. When he couldn't match their feat, his two ladies had splashed him mercilessly.

And Nick loved every moment.

"This is a God time," Maggie said, scooping another charred marshmallow into her mouth.

"A 'God' time? What do you mean, Mags?" A flush of amazement filled Nick at his niece's certainty of God's leading in her life. She sounded exactly as Shay had years ago in high school, when her faith was so strong his felt puny beside it. Lately Shay had begun to sound confident in her faith again, which made Nick very happy.

Maggie pointed up at the full moon. "That's what tonight feels like to me. Like God is here."

Shay brushed the damp curls off Maggie's forehead and hugged her. "How did you get so smart about God, Maggie?"

"My mom." Maggie peered into the night sky, her voice very soft. "She told me lots of things about how God loves us so much."

"Your mom was a smart lady, honey." Nick swallowed

hard, thrilled that Georgia's very strong faith still lived on in her child's heart.

"Grandma teaches me, too. She knows lots of stuff about God, too."

"Like what?" Nick prodded.

"Grandma said that if I had questions, I should ask God about them. So I do."

Such easy faith. A flush of shame suffused Nick that he'd ever doubted God.

"I was worried when Pastor Marty talked about God's plans for us."

"Worried?" Nick frowned. He didn't want his niece worrying about anything. "Why were you worried, Mags?" Nick asked, anxious to hear what she'd say. Shay seemed captivated, too, for she leaned forward, arms clasped around her knees and waited as Maggie assembled her thoughts, her face scrunched up with the effort.

"I couldn't figure out why He made it so I couldn't walk." Maggie's forehead furrowed. "Sometimes it's hard to understand what God's doing." She peered at Shay, her eyes earnest.

"Yes, sometimes it is very hard," Shay agreed, her face solemn.

"Grandma told me, 'You don't have to understand. You just have to work hard and trust God to do the rest.'" A huge yawn interrupted her words.

Shay snuggled Maggie against her side. "That's right, Maggie. Are you warm enough?"

"Toasty." Maggie rested her sleepy head against Shay's shoulder.

Do your part. Trust God to do the rest.

Nick suddenly felt himself getting angry. *Trust God to do the rest.* Wasn't that what he was doing? He believed that job had come from God. So why didn't he feel at peace?

He faced the same quandary with Shay. He cared so deeply

for her, but the thought of promising her anything and then failing her—something inside him twisted into a knot.

He just couldn't, wouldn't do that.

"I think Maggie's asleep," Shay murmured. When he didn't answer, she looked at him. "Why are you so quiet, Nick? Are you okay?"

"I'm thinking about what Maggie said."

"In regard to your dad?" Shay asked. "You told me once that you wanted to reconcile with him, that you hoped you would someday be able to rebuild a bond with him."

"I'm not hoping for that anymore, Shay," Nick told her grimly.

"Why not?" Her wide emerald eyes brimmed with innocence.

"Because my father doesn't want anything to do with any of us." The words spilled out of him with an acrid bitterness Nick hadn't realized he still clung to.

"You don't know that," Shay protested.

"Actually I do know that." Nick didn't want to risk Maggie hearing this so he lifted her from Shay's arms and carried her to the truck, where he settled her on the backseat. After ensuring he had a clear line of vision to the truck, he returned to Shay. He stabbed at the fire viciously as he sat down, struggling to tamp down his anger.

"Nick—" Shay touched his arm for a moment, her eyes brimming with empathy.

"You can't tell Mom any of this." He locked her gaze with his. "Not one word."

"Okay." She looked mystified by his harsh tone.

"After Georgia's death, I hired the same private investigator that tailed you in New York to find my father."

Shay's eyes widened but Nick kept going. Better to get it all out in the open.

"I thought that surely, after all these years, he'd be over

whatever he'd been going through, that he'd finally want to know us, his family." He snorted his derision. "Turns out I couldn't have been more wrong."

"Oh, Nick." Shay scooted closer so she could slide her hand into his. "I'm sorry."

"Yeah." He exhaled. "He said he had his own life now." He threaded his fingers through hers. "My father," he said, enunciating the words, "didn't want the responsibility of a family and never had, even though he had five kids. It didn't matter that we're all grown now, that we didn't want anything except to know our father. He said he'd made a clean break when he walked away years ago and he had no regrets."

Shay said nothing, simply held his hand. But Nick could feel her comfort as a tangible thing. Perhaps that was why he had to say it all, to release the pain in one torrent of bitterness. Maybe then he could heal. Maybe.

"I tried to show him pictures of his grandchildren," Nick muttered. "But he pushed them away. Can you imagine not wanting to know Maggie?"

"No, I can't imagine that," Shay whispered. "It's his loss, but we should feel sorry for him."

"Sorry?" Rage burned in Nick's heart. "Why?"

"Because your father hasn't the slightest clue as to what he threw away." Shay leaned in so her face was inches from his. "He has no idea that he has a wonderful son, a son who gives deeply of himself to others. A son the whole town is proud to call their own."

"Thanks," Nick said, looking away from her as if he didn't believe what she was saying.

"Don't thank me. It's true, Nick." Shay grasped his chin and turned his face toward hers. "The fact that your father doesn't get it, even after all these years, is sad. But it's no reflection on you. Let it go."

"I don't know if I can," he admitted.

"You have to. Hate is corrosive. It will ruin your life." Her fingers brushed his chin.

"But he—"

"God has blessed you with a wonderful family, with a community where you are appreciated." Her voice softened. "Think about that, and leave your father to God."

As Nick stared into Shay's eyes, the longing to kiss her grew until it was an ache that had to be satisfied. He leaned forward and covered her lips with his, seeking the comfort she offered, but asking for more than that. Asking for a response that would show she felt the same rush of joy that he did whenever they were together.

He felt her still then felt the slight tremble ripple through her. He shifted to move away, but then she was kissing him back, her hand curling around his neck, moving into the kiss, gently, without fear. She tasted of toasted marshmallow. Her skin felt soft as silk against his five o'clock shadow.

When Nick finally pulled back, Shay wore a bemused look.

"You're the best friend I ever had, Shay."

"Me, too," Shay said in a slightly choked tone.

Friend. But he ached to be so much more than that.

When Shay shivered, Nick wrapped an arm around her and drew her against his side. They sat there silent.

"The team wants me to start work a month early."

"Oh?" Shay's body tensed.

"They've offered a really good bonus if I show up a month early."

"In two weeks," she whispered. "After the Fourth of July."

"Yes."

She tipped her head to study him. "Will you go?"

"I don't have a choice." She didn't argue but still Nick felt he had to defend his decision. "Mom needs a new car. The old one's ready for the scrap heap, but her pension check won't stretch enough for a new one. I can't leave her with an unreliable vehicle."

"No." Shay said nothing else. But she didn't move away either. Was it because she was comfortable with him? Because she knew she could trust him?

But *should* she trust him if he was just going to leave?

"What else?" she whispered.

"Cara needs to get out of that apartment and into a house where the twins can thrive, but her husband just got laid off."

"Oh," Shay murmured.

Nick could feel her withdrawing.

"It's not that I want to leave Hope," he tried to explain. "But I can't take the risk of trying to start a new business or waiting for a job to find me. I'm the one my family depends on."

"Your mom depends on God," Shay reminded in a soft but firm tone.

"Yes, and God uses me to help her. These past months— you've become a lot more than just a friend, Shay. You've helped my mom and my niece. And me," he added with a smile. "I really wish I could stick around." *Maybe if I stayed long enough I could figure out how to have a relationship with you.* "I'd like that more than anything."

"You're a lot more than a friend to me, too, Nick." She bit her lip, lifted her head and stared into his eyes. "I care about you more than I have ever cared for anyone but Dad." She touched his cheek.

This woman had his heart. He couldn't bear to think about leaving her.

"Lots of people have long-distance relationships." Her whisper warmed his heart—how he wanted more with this special woman.

"I don't think I'm one of those people, Shay," he said, wishing it wasn't true with every fiber of his being.

"Why?" Her fingers curled into his as she met his gaze head-on, her green eyes swirling with questions.

"I'm terrible at relationships." He shook his head when she smiled. "I'm serious, Shay. You and I—we've always been friends." He gulped. "But there's a lot you don't know about me."

"I doubt that. You're the most trustworthy person I know." She leaned her head on his shoulder.

Nick's heart almost burst at the vulnerability he saw on Shay's face. Vulnerable, yet she trusted him enough to bare her heart to him. He had to be honest with her. She deserved nothing less that the complete truth.

"Tell me," she invited.

So Nick did. He told her about his last two relationships and how he'd failed to be who the person he'd loved said she needed.

"I'm just like my father," he said, his teeth grinding as he got the words out. "I don't want to be, but when push comes to shove, I get cold feet, just like he did, and rather than risk making a mess down the road, I walk out before I hurt someone."

Shay was silent for such a long time, he finally turned his head to look at her. She was grinning.

"This isn't funny," he said.

"Yes, it is, Nick. It's very funny that you of all people—Mr. Responsible—would think that you failed someone. It would never happen," she said. "Not if the moon turned purple. Not if we had a month of Sundays. Not even if someone mistreated you. It just isn't in you to dump your responsibilities."

Nick stared at her. He opened his mouth to argue but Shay shook her head.

"Impossible," she said. "I know you."

"You don't understand. You haven't even heard the details yet."

"Details don't matter. I know who you are inside." She shifted so she was facing him, her eyes flashing.

Nick thought he could lose himself in those eyes.

"I know you, Nick Green. I know how seriously you take your obligations. If your relationships ended then it was because there was something wrong with the relationships themselves, not with you. You don't walk out, Nick. Not on anybody. Not ever." She smiled again, and he felt warm all over. "You have an abundance of integrity. I'd trust you with my life."

"Did I hear you right?" Nick blinked. "You *trust* me?"

"Yep. Weird, isn't it?' Shay grinned a wicked smile then threw her arms around his neck and kissed him with a carefree abandon he'd wished for only in his dreams—until now.

Nick kissed her right back. If Shay Parker wanted to kiss him, he wasn't about to turn her down.

But, Good Lord, what happens next?

Chapter Eleven

"Happy Fourth of July!"

Shay stood on Main Street watching the parade, waving her little flag in one hand while the other was firmly tucked into Nick's. She couldn't remember when she'd been happier.

She'd made him dinner several nights in a row. He'd treated her to pizza and Mexican food. They'd shared campfires and walks and another evening at the lake, just the two of them. And they'd talked. My, how they'd talked—about everything— except the future.

Shay had skirted around the subject, longing for Nick to tell her he couldn't leave her, but purposely not asking about his decision. Staying in Hope had to be Nick's decision and though she desperately wanted him to say he was staying, she would just have to wait for his decision and keep praying about it.

She'd put her trust in God to find a way for Nick to stay.

The bubble of Shay's perfect world burst when the sound of gunshot cracked through the laughter surrounding her. For an instant, fear perched on her shoulder and told her to be afraid. But Shay was no longer a novice.

She squeezed her eyes closed and repeated a newly memorized verse.

For I hold you by your right hand, I the Lord your God. And I say to you, "Don't be afraid. I am here to help you."

Shay repeated it twice then opened her eyes just as an old model T huffed and puffed past them and continued down the parade route.

"I think that thing backfires once every parade. Are you okay?" Nick leaned past Maggie to ask, obviously sensing something amiss.

"Everything's perfect," she said and smiled. It was true. Everything *was* perfect.

The day was gorgeous, one of those not-too-hot summer days that had a soft breeze to fan you. This year the parade was on time, marching bands and cheerleaders filling the air with excitement. Maggie's joy in each entry reminded Shay of the many times she'd come here with her father and she took a moment to savor the memory.

But it was the seniors' float that made Maggie dance and point, her anticipation visible.

"Grandma, Grandma!" she called, waving her little flag and jumping up and down. "Throw me a candy. Please, Grandma."

Shay chuckled when the entire float of seniors aimed their goodies in Maggie's direction, forcing the little girl to use the hem of her blouse like an apron to collect her treats.

Just behind the seniors, someone began to sing "America The Beautiful." When it was finished Nick touched her shoulder.

"Is perfect too strong a word to describe today?" he murmured into her ear, his hand resting against her waist.

"I think it's a perfect word for a perfect day," she told him, loving the gentle yet strong support he provided.

Then her cell phone rang. She glanced at the number and swallowed. *Don't be afraid.*

"Anything urgent?" Nick asked.

"I didn't expect the New York detectives to call me again. I'll just be a minute." She stepped away to find some quiet.

But it was a very long minute, and when it was over, Shay wished she had left her phone at home.

"You missed most of the parade, but at least you won't miss lunch." Nick grinned when she returned. He helped Maggie stand then frowned at Shay's nonresponse. "Shay? What's wrong?"

"I, um, I can't go for lunch right now. The detectives in New York are faxing something they want me to look at."

"Not a problem. We'll swing by the police station on our way to Mom's. Okay?" He waited for her nod while Maggie got settled into her crutches. Then they walked to his truck. After only a few steps, Maggie gladly relinquished her bag that brimmed with goodies thrown to her from the floats in the parade.

"Didn't Grandma look nice on that float?" she said.

"Very nice," Nick agreed.

"I like the dress Shay helped her find. And I'm glad you helped them get their float working, Uncle Nick. Grandma said they wouldn't have been in the parade this year without you."

Shay grinned at him. "Always on hand to help out, aren't you?"

"It was just a motor thing. No big deal." He avoided her knowing look.

"It is a big deal for the seniors," she said. She was about to reiterate that a lot of people in Hope needed Nick when Buddy from the grocery store called out to her.

"Nice article, Shay. Looks like Whispering Hope Clinic is a real success!" he said.

"What article?" Nick asked.

"Remember Ben Marks and all the photos he took that day at the clinic? The paper must have run the story today."

And maybe, Shay mused, it would be enough to persuade Nick he was needed here. That's what she'd been praying for. "Can we stop at the store and pick up a copy? Your mom did say she needed some whipped cream for her strawberry pie," she reminded.

"Right." Nick lifted Maggie into her seat then paused. "What about the police station?"

"Oh, right." This was a holiday—Shay didn't want to be the damper. "Why don't you and Maggie go to the store and I'll meet you at your mom's place as soon as I'm finished?"

"You don't want me there?" Nick frowned. "It's not a problem."

"Nothing is ever a problem for you, is it?" Shay squeezed his hand. "But you know what? I think I'm ready to face this on my own. I feel like I have to."

"You don't have to. Just give me a few minutes to get Maggie—"

"Nick." Shay smiled and shook her head. "I need to do this. I need to stand on my own two feet. It's time." *Actually, it's past time,* she thought.

He studied her for a long moment but finally nodded.

"Okay. I'll be praying," he promised.

"Thank you. That I will gladly accept." She waved at Maggie then set off at a crisp walk across the town square toward the police services building, needing the exercise to help work off the nervous energy that filled her.

Perfect love casts out all fear.

With her shoulders back and her courage high, Shay walked into the station. Moments later Chief Dan Burger ushered her into his office.

"I've been briefed by the New York police, Miss Parker. What they'd like you to do is look at this picture and see if you recognize this person." He handed her a sheet of paper as he sat and motioned for her to do the same.

Shay looked down and inhaled sharply. He was facing the camera, smiling as if he had not a care in the world. He looked like an ordinary man.

"Miss Parker?"

"I know him," she said.

"So who is he?" The chief leaned forward, pen in hand, poised to take down her information.

"That's the thing," she whispered as a cold, clammy sweat began to form under her bangs. "I know him—that is, I'm familiar with this face. He was on the set of a number of shoots I did. But I have no idea who he is. I don't believe I ever knew his name or what, exactly, he did. I just—know him." She bit her lip. "I wish I could tell you more."

"Don't worry about it." The relaxed tone of the chief's voice calmed Shay. "Can I ask you something? I'm just curious. What was this guy doing on the set? Can you recall?"

Shay began to shake her head but Dan leaned forward.

"Close your eyes for a moment and see yourself there. What are you doing?"

"I'm in the makeup chair," she said.

"Someone's doing your hair?"

"Yes. It's a shoot of evening gowns. Very formal. I have to wear an up-do and it's not quite right. I had some sparkly clips—they're missing." She gasped, opened her eyes. "He must have been somebody's assistant because Mario, my hair guy, yelled at him to find those clips."

"I see." Dan tented his fingers. "Did this guy work with Mario?"

"No. Mario worked alone. He always made me look beautiful. So did Cerise, my makeup artist." Shay got lost in her thoughts of those hectic, frantic hours when nothing mattered more than giving the client the very best picture she could. She didn't want to model anymore, but she didn't resent it because it paid for her education and everything she had. Modeling had allowed her to come home to Hope.

"Could the guy have worked for her, this Cerise?"

"I don't know. Maybe. She always had someone cleaning her kits, her brushes. But I don't remember *him* doing it." She stared at the picture, chilled. "Is he the stalker?"

"For now, he's just a person of interest."

"I see." She had a hunch the chief wasn't going to tell her any more. "Well, I'm sorry I couldn't help more."

"You've done fine. I'll relay what you've told me to New York and they'll take it from here." He shook her hand. "But if you remember anything else, you let me know."

"Of course," she promised.

"And Ms. Parker? I can't tell you how much that clinic you work in means to this town. I know how hard it is to keep folks in a place where medical services aren't up to par. Whispering Hope has become a tremendous asset. It's even drawing people to get help for their children."

"That's what we hoped for." A rush of satisfaction surged inside and almost dislodged the unsettled feeling that photo had left her with. Almost.

"Listen, tell Nick I said thanks, will you? My mother's been nagging me to get her golf cart fixed for ages. He did it in about ten minutes at the seniors' hall when they had their fix-it time last Saturday morning. Saved me another bungled attempt with the thing." He scratched his chin. "There are plenty of regular folks who'd pay him good money if he could get some of their broken-down stuff going."

"Really?" That caught Shay's attention.

"Sure. I was talking to some of the guys on council. They wish he'd open a shop. He'd never have a spare minute."

"I will tell him what you said," Shay promised. "I've been trying to talk him into staying. After all, his mom and his niece are here. But Nick thinks that the work he does in town wouldn't support a business. He feels he has to go back to Seattle to earn a living."

"Well." The chief rubbed his head. "I don't suppose he'd earn a pro-ball salary in Hope, but then it doesn't cost as much to live here either." His eyes narrowed and he seemed to get lost in thought.

"I'd better get going. Nick's mom is planning a big July Fourth barbecue and I don't want to be late." She pushed the photo toward him, less than eager to look at that face again, and stood up. "I hope they catch the right guy."

"Yeah. Creeps like that think they can get away with their nasty tricks, but sooner or later they get found out. God has a way of evening things up. Maybe not on our timetable, but always on His."

"Thanks, Chief." Shay left, lost in thought as she walked back through the town square, got in her car and drove to the Green home.

She couldn't help brooding over the picture she'd seen. The familiarity of that face struck her, but she couldn't recall exactly why. Despite the many Scriptures she recited as she drove, an aura of disquiet rattled her nerves. She was glad when she arrived at Nick's and hurried to the backyard, where laughter spilled over the fence.

Shay stood still, soaking in the happy atmosphere. Friends and neighbors filled the yard, laughing while kids played games. Maggie, moving as best she could now that she was using canes, was the life of the party.

Shay's observant eye noted that the little girl was almost lifting the canes up so she could go faster, proving that the strength in her legs was almost normal. In a very short time, Maggie would be walking without aid.

"You're back." Nick wound an arm around her waist. "Everything okay with the police?"

"I'll tell you later," she said sotto voce. "I don't want to spoil the afternoon."

"You couldn't." He grinned as his mother, conned by the kids, took a turn—and failed—at flying a kite. "I don't think anything could put a damper on this day. It's time to celebrate, Shay. Want a frank?"

"And some lemonade. You do have lemonade?" she asked, one eyebrow arched.

"Is the sun shining?" He drew her forward into the circle of people he'd been talking with.

Shay accepted compliments about the paper's feature on the clinic. When she saw Nick busy manning the grill, she found a quiet corner inside and sat down to read the newspaper article for herself.

"It's good, isn't it? Bob covers how the clinic idea started with Jessica's illness, and how it's grown and is now impacting people from here and far away." Jaclyn sat down across from her. "It's also very good publicity for you and the results you've achieved for your clients."

"I guess." Shay closed the newspaper with a sigh. "I was hoping for more."

"More?" Jaclyn looked surprised. "More of what?"

"I was hoping he would write about Nick and the roly-poly, the Tiger, the giggle machine…" She met Jaclyn's inquiring look. "I've been trying to persuade Nick that Hope needs him more than Seattle does."

"Because?"

"Because I want him to stay. Because I'm in love with him, Jaclyn." Saying the words solidified something inside, made her feelings more real.

"In love—wow." Jaclyn grinned. "You told me, several times I might add, that it was only friendship between you. I didn't expect love to develop this soon."

"Neither did I." She sighed. "And I can't see how it is going to work out."

"Because he doesn't care about you?" Jaclyn asked, her voice soft.

"I think he does care about me."

"So what's the problem?" Her friend frowned. "Oh. You're still feeling skittish?"

"No." Shay blinked in surprise. "I'm not like that around Nick. I was at first, but now—I guess I'm learning to trust him."

"Oh, that's wonderful! I'm so glad, honey." Jaclyn hugged her then returned to her seat.

"It is an amazing feeling. The only thing is, I don't know what can come of it." Shay told her about Nick's determination to leave and about her visits with the police. "Even if he stayed, I'm not much of a bargain. Seems like I still have to fight back the fear every step of the way."

"At least you are fighting. That's a huge step." Jaclyn frowned when she didn't reply. "Something else is troubling you?"

"I've been studying with Nick's mom. She's shown me that I have to learn to trust God. And I'm trying. I really am. But—"

"But you feel that maybe He has abandoned you? Or forgotten you?" Jaclyn asked.

"It sounds juvenile, I know. But after all the verses I've learned, all the praying and Bible studying I've done, I thought I'd feel empowered or not so alone or—something. But I don't." Shay stared at her hands. "I keep praying, I keep reading the verses, but it's beginning to seem like I'm only going through the motions. Like today, looking at that picture, even though I was inside the police station—the fear still rises up."

Jaclyn remained silent, listening as Shay released her pent-up feelings.

"Look around at all the love in this home. You and Kent are making your family together. Brianna and Zac are doing the same. I know beyond a shadow of a doubt that what you all have is exactly what I want." Tears welled but she dashed them away. "But I'm beginning to doubt I'll ever get it. Especially if Nick leaves."

"You've always talked about having a family. You said you trusted Nick. Now you have to trust God, too, because He knows what your heart desires." Jaclyn shook her blond head. "Nothing works without trusting God, Shay. Do that, then go for it. Go for the heart. Nothing else is good enough for you. Just remember, Nick will never be able to guarantee you safety. Nobody can."

"I know. That's why I have to get this fear thing sorted out, so that I'll be whole and able to love in return. Only—" She bit her lip, unwilling to voice her thoughts.

"Only it would be easier if Nick actually said he loves you and he's staying in Hope?" Jaclyn finished.

"Yes."

"I wish I could tell you there's some kind of easy way to guarantee he will, but the truth is, there isn't." Jaclyn shrugged. "It all comes back to faith. I think the way to put your faith into action, in this case, is to cherish whatever moments you have with Nick, put yourself on the line and tell him how you feel."

"Live with no regrets," Shay mused. "That's what my dad used to say. 'Live your best life right now.'"

"I think there's a lot of wisdom in that." Jaclyn rose. "And remember that just because you don't 'feel' different doesn't mean things aren't changing inside you. How often did our youth leaders remind us that the Christian life is founded on faith, not on feelings?"

"They taught us a lot, didn't they? And we probably didn't appreciate them enough back then." Shay rose, too, and hugged her best friend. "That's why this place is so important to me. I have a history here. I belong."

"Then live like that. Don't wait for things to change," Jaclyn advised as they strolled back outside. "Be honest with him, do what you can and trust God to handle what you can't. Now, where is that husband of mine? This music is too good to ignore."

"Blame it on Maggie. She found some of my old cassettes and insists on playing them," Nick said, walking toward them. "I wondered where you'd disappeared to. Want to dance?" he asked Shay.

Shay waved as Jaclyn headed toward Kent. While they'd been talking, the sun had set and candlelit paper lanterns now created a soft, intimate glimmering in the backyard. A pretty ballad about love floated through the evening air. Shay turned toward Nick with a smile. "Your music? But this isn't that awful hard rock you used to love."

"It wasn't that I loved that music as much as I fancied myself a guitarist back then." Nick held out a hand and led Shay to a back corner of the yard covered with beautifully fragrant tea roses. No one else was there. "I don't think we've danced together since prom night. I'll try not to step on your toes." His arm closed around her waist and his hand enveloped hers.

"I don't mind," she said.

I don't mind? What an understatement.

In Nick's arms, swaying to the music, with laughter and love of his family and friends surrounding them, it felt intimately right to be sharing this moment. Jaclyn was right, Shay mused. The Bible said God had a plan for her life. She had to trust in that and enjoy the special moments He sent her way.

"You're awfully quiet. Tired?" he asked, his breath brushing her cheek, only inches from his mouth.

"I feel wonderful," Shay told him.

"Good." He grinned. "Because if I remember right, the next song is bit more energetic."

Shay laughed with abandonment as he swung her wide and then pulled her back to him. Though she'd forgotten some of the old moves, Nick remembered all their favorite steps. Soon they had drawn a crowd of onlookers who clapped them on to an exuberant finish.

Flushed and slightly embarrassed, Shay tucked her arm in Nick's and bowed at their applause but shook her head when he inclined his to ask if she wanted to continue.

"Too thirsty," she told him.

"And you haven't sampled any of my fantastic burgers," he said. "Actually, I didn't either. I was too busy cooking. I'm starving. Let's go see what Mom's got left."

The buffet table was, in usual Green style, loaded. They helped themselves. Nick snagged two Adirondack chairs that had wide enough arms to hold their heaping plates and the tinkling glasses of lemonade he brought.

"You're not supposed to eat the watermelon first," he said, eyebrows lowered in a fake scowl when she took a bite from the triangle of red fruit.

"Who says?" Shay munched happily on her watermelon.

"I do." He reached out with his napkin and dabbed at a trickle of juice dribbling down her chin. "It messes up such a pretty face."

"Pffffft to pretty faces," she told him and blew a raspberry to emphasize her words. "Life is about so much more than a pretty face."

"You seem different tonight." Nick set aside his plate and studied her. "Something happen that you want to tell me about?"

Shay took a few moments to tell Nick about what had happened at the police station and about her conversation with Jaclyn. "I guess I've decided I'm going to get out of the control seat and leave things up to God." She laughed when Nick blew his own raspberry. "Go ahead, laugh. But I have decided. Being here tonight, seeing the love your mom shows everyone has been a real eye-opener to me. She went through such tough times when your dad left. Her arthritis is getting worse, yet she faces each day with abundant joy and love. She's on top of her circumstances because she trusts God, always. That's where I want to be."

"I thought the newspaper article showed you were already there." Nick sipped his lemonade thoughtfully.

"The newspaper article showed what my clients have achieved," she corrected. "What needs to happen inside me isn't for the newspaper."

"Uncle Nick?" Maggie stood in front of them, holding her canes. "Are you sure we can't have the fireworks?"

"We talked about it, Mags. You know the fire chief said we're too close to other houses. I'm sorry." Nick ruffled the little girl's hair.

"But my place isn't too close to other houses." Shay winked at Maggie before she turned to Nick. "Do you think we could set off the fireworks at my place? Do you even know how to set off fireworks anymore?"

"Please." He shot her an offended look that said she should know better than to ask. "We'd need to hook up a hose, in case any grass caught. That rain last week helped, but the monsoon season hasn't really soaked anything enough to be fully safe yet."

"I have hoses. And lots of water," Shay told him. "But I don't want to drag anyone away from your mom's party. Look at her. She's having a ball."

Mrs. Green tipped back her head and laughed at something Ned Barns said. She was flushed, her smile beaming.

"We'll wait until everyone leaves," Nick said. "Then, when everything's cleaned up, we'll go."

"But I'll get too tired and fall asleep. Then I'll miss everything," Maggie wailed.

"If you go to your room and rest now, I promise I'll wake you up when it's time to go to Shay's." Nick squatted in front of her. "But no fuss and no telling Grandma. She's enjoying herself, and that's what we want. Right?"

"Right." Maggie high-fived him then grinned at Shay.

Two hours later the three of them stood in the desert, waiting for the time-delay mechanism to click and ignite the first in the series of fireworks Nick had set up. Finally it did. Noise burst across the desert and flares of color lit the night sky as rocket after rocket exploded.

"It's not a meteor shower," Nick murmured in Shay's ear. "But Maggie seems to be enjoying it."

"So am I." Shay was very conscious—too conscious—of his arm draped around her shoulders. She couldn't help wondering if he'd kiss her tonight. Memories of their evening at the pond and a rush of feelings bubbling inside made her catch her breath.

She knew now that she loved Nick, loved him with everything she possessed. She wanted to spend her days by his side, to push into the future with him, to share Maggie and his mom and all the happy moments family could bring. He was still her very best friend, but now he'd become much more than that.

If only she could know if he felt the same. Did he love her?

"Here it comes, the grand finale," Nick said. "Make sure you don't fall asleep, Maggie-mine."

"I won't." Maggie sat on the lawn chair Shay had provided, her eyes huge as she watched the display.

"Happy Fourth of July," Nick murmured in her ear.

"Happy—" Shay never got to finish her sentence because

Nick's lips touched hers. Her heart exploded as his lips moved over hers and he pulled her into his embrace. She let herself melt into him as she kissed him back, pouring her feelings into that kiss, pleading silently with him to say the words that she desperately wanted to hear. That he wasn't going to Seattle next week. That he wasn't going away at all. Ever.

This, she prayed when Nick finally ended the kiss by turning her to stand in front of him and looping his arms around her waist, *is what I want, Lord. Please let him love me. Please let him decide to stay.*

Nick, however, said nothing.

Chapter Twelve

"Is that what you wanted?" Nick stood back and watched Shay's newest client turn the handles of Nick's giggle machine with bandaged hands.

"Perfect." Shay assessed the movement, her emerald eyes shimmering. "Try again, Robbie, honey," she encouraged in a very soft tone.

The child complied, chuckling with delight when his actions made a clown pop up. He kept going, working a little harder after a balloon inflated. Under Shay's direction Nick tweaked the machine until it was a perfect fit for the little boy who'd been burned in a cooking fire. When Nick's phone kept interrupting, he finally switched it off.

"You're certainly getting popular," Shay said, waving goodbye as Robbie left with his mom and the precious machine. "Everybody wants Nick."

"Everybody wants Nick to fix their broken stuff," he corrected, pretending annoyance. "The Girl Scouts are coming to the seniors' hall on Saturday morning, and on Monday the Rotary Club wants help with one of their service projects. I suggested they get the seniors group to pitch in. There is a lot of knowledge there that could be tapped."

"Your mother said you're also booked for Tuesday nights."

Shay readied the room for Maggie's session, which would start once her checkup with Jaclyn was finished.

"Yeah. About that." Nick wasn't sure how this would go over. Not that Shay would ever balk at helping anyone, but she was already so busy.

"Uh-oh. That doesn't sound good." She glanced over one shoulder at him.

For the hundredth time Nick admired how stunningly beautiful Shay was. Though her work clothes—baggy cotton tops and pants that let her move easily—were hardly haute couture, Shay always looked stunning. Today she'd bundled her gorgeous hair onto the top of her head and secured it with a big comb that was the exact color of her eyes. A few wispy tendrils of richly glowing copper escaped to caress her cheeks and her long, slim neck. He got that warm feeling remembering just how perfectly his lips felt on hers.

"Nick?"

"Yeah?" He gulped and refocused.

"Are you sick?" Shay studied him with concern.

"Maybe." He stepped nearer, holding her gaze, wondering if she'd back away if he tried to kiss her. This *was* her workplace, after all, and even though no one else was here—

"Nick? Hello?" She snapped her fingers under his nose. "You *are* ill."

"No. But sometimes when I'm near you I get this weird feeling in my chest." Apparently that hadn't come out exactly the way he'd intended, because now it looked as if Shay thought he needed a defibrillator. "Uh, never mind."

"You were saying about the seniors?" Shay glanced at her watch. "You need me to step in and take over some of your classes when you leave town?"

"Not exactly."

So she was okay with him leaving? Nick ignored that for

the moment as he swallowed the golf ball in his throat. "You know how old people get."

"How they *get?*" Shay's arched eyebrows rose. Her lips twitched. "Old, do you mean?"

"No. We all get old." Now she was laughing at him. *Get a grip, Green.* "I mean stiff. Achy. Hurting. Hard to move. Joint issues. Like Mom. You know?"

"Oh." She nodded. "Yes, I do. And it's not just old people who suffer with those issues, for your information."

"Right." He was putting this so badly. "Well, I figured that maybe, if you could fit it in, because I know how busy you are now that you're working with Jaclyn on those church renovations—"

"Just say what you want, Nick."

"I want you to teach a yoga class to the seniors," he blurted. "If you know yoga, I mean. If not, maybe you could teach them some stretching exercises, stuff that will help them limber up a bit. Sort of like you did for Mom."

She stared at him for a long time, obviously suspicious about his request. He couldn't blame her. Shay knew he didn't have much time left here.

"Is that what you really want?"

"What do you mean?" Nick shifted, unable to break the hold of her gaze as it locked with his.

"I'm wondering why you're asking me."

"Uh, because you know yoga. I think."

"You just can't help it, can you? You have to help everybody. And now you're trying to draw me into it." She leaned against the parallel bars, a tiny smile tipping up her kissable lips.

"Well." No point in trying to deny it—those big eyes of hers saw everything. "Yes."

"Okay." Her smiled faded. "I guess I could teach a few yoga moves on Tuesday night, but only if you attend."

"Can do." He shifted uncomfortably. "Uh—"

Shay's eyes narrowed. After a moment she sighed. "What else?"

"I was speaking to Heddy Grange today. Her granddaughter and some other girls want to learn to play soccer. Lots of people have volunteered but no one wants to coach. So since you were captain of the soccer team in high school, I was wondering—"

"When?"

"Thursday nights?" Nick held his breath. He'd promised Heddy he'd find someone to coach. If Shay wouldn't help—

"You do realize what you're doing, don't you?" She looked up at him through her thick lashes. "You're making yourself an indispensable part of Hope. You belong here, Nick."

He hated it but he had to say it.

"I have to leave next week."

Shay stared at him.

"That's why I'm trying to get all these things settled. I want to ensure I've kept all my promises. I want to make sure everything's up and running so nobody is put out when I'm gone."

She stood there, staring at her toes for several long moments.

"I see," she whispered.

Two words and yet they so perfectly expressed her obvious disappointment in him. How he wished it could be different but he just couldn't shirk his duties to his family.

Nick wanted to wrap his arms around her and promise her he'd be back. He wanted to hold her once more, pour heart and soul into a kiss, but that wouldn't make leaving any easier.

"I have to go, Shay."

"Do you? So it was all just talk about trusting God." With a hiss of frustration, she clapped her hands on her narrow hips and glared at him. "Who do you think is going to see the needs in Hope and fill them when you leave?"

"Somebody will. I was just the—facilitator. A temporary one."

Her eyes darkened. She tried to turn away but he stopped her with a hand on her arm. "I have to leave, Shay. I need this job. Please understand."

For a moment she avoided looking at him. But when she finally did, her green eyes were glossy—with tears? For him?

"You haven't even looked for a job here," she said, her voice wobbling.

"I've spent the past six months looking for a way to remain in Hope. I've prayed about it endlessly." He put his hands on her shoulders, forcing her to look at him. "You and I both know there's no getting around this."

"Everyone's always telling *me* to have faith," she said, her green eyes turning glacial. "*You* have to have faith that God has an answer to this. We need you here, Nick."

We need you.

Shay needed him. And Nick needed her. Boy, how he needed her. He needed her in his life to give the days meaning, to share the highs and lows.

He'd tried to have faith, to believe something would come up at the last minute. But nothing had. And his mom's car was sputtering worse than ever. He needed that bonus.

"You'll all manage very well on your own." She stepped back and he let his hands drop. "I wish I could stay here, Shay. I truly do."

"Nick—" She stood staring at him, her brows drawn together in a troubled frown. Her hand reached out to touch his cheek, stayed a second longer, then fell to her side.

His gut clenched with wanting, but he fought back.

"You're getting your fear under control, Shay. Whispering Hope Clinic is on the rise, just as Jessica would have wanted." Nick lowered his voice, trying to make her see the truth without revealing how hard this was for him. "Your kids will heal and walk and run because this is where you belong, here, helping them."

"I love you, Nick."

Her words shocked him into silence.

"I have for a while. If I've fought my fear, it's because of you, because you stood with me through the worst of it, because you showed me I am not alone." She stood straight and tall. She'd never looked more beautiful to him. "It's you, Nick, with your nightly visits to my place to make sure I'm safe, who has made me feel I was secure and that I could trust again."

He hadn't realized she'd known about that.

"You make me laugh, Nick, and you help me when I cry. You cheer me on when I want to give up. You hold me up when I stumble," she whispered. "You helped me face the worst issue in my past, and you're here now, helping me again. I love you for all of that."

"Shay, don't." He couldn't bear to hear her say those words.

"Why? I'm only telling the truth. Hope and I have both changed because of you. You make us see what we could be." She folded her arms across herself as if to shield her body. "You, Hope, me—we're perfectly matched. God has a place for you here. If only you could see that, you'd understand that you can't leave. You can't give up on us."

"If God has a way for me to be here, I'm totally open to it." A twinge of bitterness prickled inside. "But so far I'm not seeing it."

"Because you want God to show you before you'll trust Him." Shay's smile held sympathy, understanding, sadness. "You know the most important thing I've learned since I've started facing my fears? Faith is just that—faith. Faith is when you don't see a way and you don't see how you can get through. You don't even see a sign that what you hope for is possible. But you believe anyway. You trust God to work it out."

Maggie opened the door and walked in, thumping her canes on the floor.

Nick did a double take. Maggie wasn't really using those canes—she was walking totally on her own strength. Shay smiled at his surprise.

"Hey, Maggie." She took the canes and set them aside. "Today our whole time is going to be spent without these because you don't need them anymore, sweetie."

Maggie whooped with joy. Nick stood on the sidelines watching while they worked, his heart in his throat as his niece completed every exercise without any help or support. At first her steps seemed hesitant, but as she adjusted her balance and gained confidence she moved more easily. By the end of the session, she was triumphant and flushed with success.

"Now, wasn't that worth all the hard work?" Shay asked with a grin.

"Yes! Thank you, Shay." Maggie wrapped her arms around Shay's legs.

"Don't thank me. You're the one who believed in yourself and hung on to that belief even when it hurt and you didn't feel like doing it anymore." She drew the little girl away so she could hunker down to her level. "I'm very proud of you, Maggie."

"I'm proud of me, too."

Shay laughed and hugged Maggie. As Nick watched the two embrace, he felt left out. This was what he'd miss when he left, this intimacy, this closeness, this sharing.

This love.

Shay's love.

He didn't want to go. He couldn't stay.

"We can't forget to thank Uncle Nick either," Shay reminded. "All those amazing machines he made for you really helped your recovery."

"Thank you, Uncle Nick." Maggie walked slowly toward him, standing straight and tall, brown eyes shining with joy. She held up her arms as she had so often in the past months.

Nick swung her into his arms and hugged her close to his heart, his throat choked with thanksgiving and joy and love.

"You're so welcome, Maggie-mine."

Over Maggie's head he caught Shay watching them. Her gaze locked with his, and after a long moment she nodded as if to say, *This is the kind of faith I'm talking about.*

He wanted to believe. He wanted to have that kind of faith. But—

He couldn't do it. He couldn't give up his only means of security for a faint hope that somehow, someway, sometime, something would come along that he could depend on. He needed more than hope.

Maggie wiggled and he set her down. "I love you, Mags. You know that."

"I know, Uncle Nick. I love you, too." She leaned in and kissed his cheek. "I couldn't have walked without you."

"You would have," he told her, tweaking her nose. "You would have found a way."

"But I didn't have to, 'cause God sent you."

God sent him? Nick couldn't wrap his mind around that.

"I want you to sit down, Maggie, because I have a few things I need to say to you." Shay pulled forward a child-size chair and waited until Maggie was seated. Then she folded herself on the floor in the Lotus position. "You have done amazingly well. But I want you to remember that your body gets tired. When it does, you use this." She held out one of the small canes.

"But—" Maggie's face pinched tight "—I'm better."

"You are. But your body is still healing. Some days it will be tired. That's when you use the canes."

"I won't get tired." Maggie's stubborn tone made Shay shake her head.

"I know what I'm talking about, sweetheart. I helped you get this far, didn't I?"

"Yes."

"Then listen to me now and trust me," she said with a sideways look at Nick. "You walk as much as you want, but take a rest when you get tired, just like you did with the exercises."

"I won't get tired." She thrust out her determined chin. "I'm strong."

"Maggie." Shay took her hands and held them, her voice compelling. "God made your body and He did an excellent job. But He made it to work and to rest, to play *and* to sleep."

From Nick's viewpoint, Maggie remained unconvinced.

"You said God healed you," Shay said.

"He did." Maggie had no doubt.

"So are you going to undo all His work, ruin His gift, by trying to get your own way?" Shay leaned forward. "I'm not trying to punish you, Maggie. I'm trying to tell you what to expect and how to be prepared for it. You know I'm your friend."

"Okay." Maggie heaved a heavy sigh. "I'll do what you say. I promise."

"Good. And if you are still feeling strong and haven't overdone it, I'll have a surprise for you on Saturday afternoon."

"Really?"

Shay grinned as Maggie plied her with a thousand questions, but she offered no further clues. "Saturday afternoon," was all she would say.

As Nick watched Maggie leave the workout room, he couldn't find the words with which to thank Shay. Anything he thought of seemed too small, too simple to express his gratitude. But he said it anyway.

"Thank you."

"You're the one who inspired her to keep going." Shay walked to the door with him, both of them watching Maggie navigating the hall.

Near the far end the little girl paused. Several moments passed before she transferred her cane to her other hand and leaned on it. Then she glanced back over one shoulder.

"Good girl," Shay murmured.

"Will she need to come back?" he asked.

"I'd like to see her twice more this week, just to make sure everything is fine." Shay held his gaze. "Then once a week for a month after that, barring anything unforeseen. I'll call your mother with the appointment times."

Because he wouldn't be here. Anger made him say, "It's not as if I'm choosing to go, Shay."

"Aren't you?" She touched his arm so he would look at her. "I love you, Nick," she said in a very soft but clear voice. "I think you have feelings for me, too. You couldn't kiss me the way you have unless you did." She touched his cheek with her fingertips. "I believe that together, with God's help, we could do something wonderful here in Hope. But you're afraid to take a chance on me and on God's ability to provide for you."

"I'm not afraid," he denied.

Shay let her hand drop to her side. "What do you call it?"

"Duty to my family. Obligation. Sense."

"All excuses," she said. "Faith doesn't have excuses. It simply says 'I believe.'"

"And we're back to where we started, Shay—where this conversation always starts. How will I provide for my family if I don't have work?" he demanded, irritated that she wouldn't see this from his perspective, as if he wanted to leave.

"The same way you've always provided for them." Her voice dropped to a whisper when Maggie looked back at them. "You'll ask God to help them and you, and then you'll get on with doing what you can with whatever God gives you."

"It's not that simple, Shay."

"But you see," she said with a smile, "it is. You either trust, or you don't. That's what your mother taught me. It all starts with a choice." She lifted her hand and waved as Ted passed Maggie at the end of the hall. "Hi, Ted. Come on in. I've been waiting for you."

"It's all very clear for you, isn't it, Shay?"

"I'm a work in progress," Shay replied, angling her head toward Maggie, who waited at the end of the hall. "Like her. Like all of us. But I will get there. God will get me there if I continue to put my faith in Him. He has plans for me."

Shay ushered Ted into her workroom and gently closed the door, leaving Nick standing there. Feeling bereft and more alone than he had ever been, Nick walked toward Maggie as he struggled to assimilate Shay's words with what he knew in his heart.

He had to leave, to take that job, to build security for his family.

But oh, how he longed to stay and accomplish all the things Shay spoke of.

She loved him. How could that be? The wonder of it simply didn't compute.

Did he dare imagine that God had used Maggie's horrible accident to draw the two of them together because He meant for them to share a future? Maybe even a family?

Finally he dared imagine it. A family with Shay, sharing each day, each trial, each joy. Impromptu picnics with Maggie, face-to-face chats with his mom and Shay, by his side. Always.

Are all things really possible, God?

Chapter Thirteen

"What's the surprise, Shay?" Maggie's eyes sparkled with excitement as she almost danced across her grandmother's front porch late Saturday morning.

Overly conscious of Nick sprawled on a chaise longue behind her and swamped by a rush of love that threatened to swamp her, Shay hid her emotions by hugging his mother. It hurt so much to be so near him and not go to him, not wrap her arms around him and tell him that she loved him. But nothing had changed. She whispered a prayer for help.

"How are you, Mrs. Green?" she asked.

"Never better, my dear. I don't know how to thank you for your hard work with Maggie." She dabbed at the tear forming in the corner of her eye. "To see her walking again is a total answer to prayer."

"Yes, it is. A special answer to a little girl's faith." Shay squeezed her hand then turned toward Maggie. "Sneakers, jeans, jacket—check?"

"Check. And cane." Maggie held it up. A burst of barking from Shay's car made her eyes widen. "Are we taking Hugs?"

"Your uncle said he'd look after him while we're gone." Shay's face burned. She explained that Hugs had escaped his pen and found his way into her closet, where he'd chosen an expensive pair of silver Versace shoes—her favorite—to chew on. For peace of mind and the safety of her wardrobe, she'd asked Nick to watch him while she was away with Maggie today.

Nick made several jokes at her expense and then suggested she'd have to figure out another solution for the dog while she was at work, but she sensed he was keeping things light as a way of withdrawing from her, because he didn't like what she'd said the other day.

Shay couldn't help that. All she could do was pray he'd see the truth and put his trust and faith in God to supply his needs.

"Major and I have several events planned for today," Nick said.

"Major?" Shay lifted one eyebrow. "Who or what is Major?"

"That's my name for your distinguished animal."

"Uh-huh." She watched him balance his coffee cup on his flat midriff and asked, "Events such as—?"

"A nap is first on the list."

"Good luck with that." She returned to the car, put her dog on a leash and led him to the house. "Under any circumstance, do not let this animal into your house," she said to Mrs. Green as she handed the lead to Nick. "He is death to expensive clothing."

"Well, I don't have any, so we should get along fine. Bye, Maggie. Be good." She wrapped her granddaughter in a hug.

"I will, Grandma. Bye, Uncle Nick." She hugged him, too, then presented herself to Shay. "I'm ready."

"Call me when you need me, Shay. And you will need me—argh!" Nick's parting shot was cut off as Hugs knocked over his coffee cup and stained his shirt.

"You'll probably be the one to call me," Shay shot back and laughed at his grumbled comment. "We'll be back before dark," she told Mrs. Green. She allowed herself one last glance at Nick before making sure Maggie was belted in. Her car started on the first turn and she drove away without looking back.

"Where are we going?" Maggie asked.

"I thought we'd head to the lake for a swim and a picnic at a special place I used to go years ago with my dad." Shay felt an inward tickle of delight. Maggie couldn't possibly know that Shay had chosen this isolated location as a test to herself, to prove she hadn't just spouted words to Nick but had truly found the trust in God she'd touted. "I love swimming."

"So do I." Maggie grinned. "And diving."

"We'll do both, I promise." She pressed the button so the roof would retract. The feel of the warm breeze against her skin made everything better. "You'll be so tired when we get home that you'll sleep for a week."

The sparkle in Maggie's eyes told Shay she intended to make those words come true.

The previous evening Shay had scouted out the road to the place her dad had called Mooney's in memory of an old silver prospector. Confident in her route, she drove to the site of their picnic, a small tree-enclosed glade that required a short hike from where they parked. Once Maggie was out of the car, Shay handed her the cane.

"Take this just in case," she said. "You can use it like a walking stick up the hill." She spared a thought to wonder if she should have chosen such a remote spot, but Maggie loved to fish and the best spot was at this secluded part of the lake. Maggie would love it when she saw the rod Shay had tucked into her rucksack.

Breathless from lugging the picnic basket uphill, Shay felt her efforts were well worth it when they arrived at the small lake. Once immersed in the water they'd have a fantastic view for miles in any direction of the desert floor below them.

When the sun grew too warm, they'd have plenty of shade under the cottonwoods that clung to the hilltop.

"I have to sit down." Maggie puffed out the words, her voice trembling.

"Okay. Sit here and rest a moment." Shay worried she'd tired the child too much. She knew better than anyone that Maggie's mobility wasn't yet back to normal. But once she'd tucked their picnic in a nearby shady spot, Maggie had found new energy. She peeled off her clothes to reveal her pretty red swimsuit beneath.

"Let's swim," she said with a giggle.

"Go slowly," Shay directed. "It's slippery in spots." Glowing with perspiration, she dragged off her own jeans and T-shirt, glad she'd put on her suit in the cool of her house. She helped Maggie over the stones and into the water. "Oh, this feels good," she breathed as she glided into the water.

Time stood still as they paddled lazily for a while. The screech of a hawk disturbed Shay's calm once and she glanced around nervously, wondering if she should have asked Nick to come. Immediately the bubble of anxiety began building.

God has not given us a spirit of fear.

Shay let the words swell and fill her mind as she reminded herself who was in charge. The fear ebbed. She whispered a prayer of thanksgiving just before Maggie swamped her with a cannonball splash. The little girl's squeals and giggles drove away whatever fragments remained as they played in their paradise.

When they climbed out of the water and dried off, Maggie sat on her towel while Shay laid out the feast she'd prepared. Shay was delighted as the little girl devoured her favorite foods.

"This is so fun." Maggie leaned against a tree trunk and drank her lemonade.

Shay leaned over and hugged the child who'd grown into

her heart. "You're a very special girl, Maggie." She swallowed past the lump in her throat, refusing to dwell on the thought that she might never have a daughter like Maggie, someone to hold and hold on to. Someone to love.

There were those doubts again. As if God didn't know her heart's desire.

Trust, she reminded herself.

For God has said, "I will never, never fail you nor forsake you."

"I have a surprise." Shay reached back to grab her pack and swung it in front of Maggie. "Dig in here and see if you find something."

"A surprise?" Maggie hunched over the bag. She gave a squeal as she pulled out the rod and reel. "I love fishing!" she said as she popped open the small tackle box and took out a hook.

"I think I've heard you say that once or twice." Shay grinned at the studiously bent head. A movie played in her head of fifteen years ago when Nick had insisted she learn how to fish. He'd been as intent as Maggie on setting the hook just right.

Dear Nick. Her heart pinched with longing.

Trust.

They spent the next hour fishing. Shay had been half hoping that nothing would bite because she hated taking fish off the line, but Maggie caught four. As deftly as any expert, she slid the squirming creatures off the hook and set them back into the water to live another day.

When it was time to pack up and go, Maggie said, "We should come again and bring Uncle Nick. He likes doing things with you."

Shay's breath hitched. If only—

"I wish he didn't have to go away next week," Maggie said with a mournful face.

"Well, maybe he'll come back for a visit soon," was the only thing Shay could think of to say. She wanted Nick here, too, but maybe that was just her own selfish desire. Maybe God's plan for him did lie in Seattle.

Maybe she was supposed to live alone.

"Ready to go back?" Shay asked.

"Yes." Maggie glanced around one last time. "Thank you, Shay."

"You're welcome, darling."

Shay went ahead of Maggie so she could help when needed. And help was needed because a very hard wind starting whipping across the desert floor, raising sand as it moved in gusts and whorls. The grit bit into their skin with a ferocity that surprised Shay until she saw a voluminous yellow cloud forming in the distance.

"A sandstorm is coming," she told Maggie as panic wrapped its tentacles around her heart. She threw her gear in the back of the car. "You get inside while I put the top up."

But the top wouldn't move because Shay's engine wouldn't start.

We're stuck out here, alone, and no one knows where we are.

For a moment panic rendered Shay immobile, until the slash of sand in her face jerked her back to awareness.

Shelter. They needed shelter.

She struggled to manually lift the top into place but the wind was fierce and almost ripped it out of her hand. In the midst of struggling with it, she caught sight of Maggie's face and knew she had to get the scared little girl to safety. But first she would call Nick for help. He would find them—Shay knew that as certainly as she knew her own name.

Only her cell phone had no reception.

As another blast of grit pelted her bare arms and face, Shay knew she could not delay. They had to move.

"Come on, sweetie. We'll hide in one of these caves until this passes. I'll help you." She half boosted Maggie up the first step of the incline they'd just descended. It was too rocky to carry her and risk a fall that would undo all Maggie's hard work to walk again. "There's a place here where I used to stay when Dad and I played hide-and-seek. We'll wait in there. We're going to be fine, Maggie. Don't worry."

"I'm not worried. I'm praying." Maggie's lips moved as they struggled upward.

"You stay, honey. I'm going back for some stuff," Shay said when they were finally inside. She saw Maggie's face tighten and hugged her. "Don't worry. I just want to get the rest of the food and a blanket, in case we have to camp here for a bit. You keep praying."

"I'll ask God to send Uncle Nick," Maggie said.

"Good idea." Shay paused in the opening of the cave. But how would Nick know where to find them?

The wind tore at her as she scrambled down the rocks to her car. It didn't seem to be dissipating. Moving as quickly as possible, she bundled as much as she could carry into her rucksack, including the leftover lemonade. Then she scrambled back up to the cave.

"I'm back," she called to Maggie, raising her voice to be heard over the wind. "I'm just going to step outside and try my phone again to see if I can let your grandmother know that we'll be late." She was grateful when Maggie didn't argue. If only her own faith was that strong.

Shay's heart sank when she saw there was only one bar of reception.

"Please let this work," she whispered as she dialed.

The fourth time she edged a little closer to the precipice and extended her arm. To her amazement the call went through and was immediately picked up by Nick.

"Shay, there's a bad storm…" he said, his voice fading.

"Nick!" She stretched her arm an inch farther and yelled, hoping the wind wouldn't obliterate her voice. "My car's dead. We're at Mooney's. Please help."

The phone blinked out; the battery was dead. All she could do was pray he'd heard her. She walked back into the cave slowly as she tried to come up with a way to tell Maggie she wasn't sure when help was coming. What were they going to do? If she could carry Maggie out, they might get caught in a rainstorm and that meant getting wet and risking hypothermia when the desert cooled off as it always did at night. They wouldn't have enough clothes to keep warm even if they snuggled together inside the cave. Rattlers came out at night. Javelina pigs and mountain lions stalked and fed at night.

They were in trouble.

"I'm c-cold, Shay." Maggie sat huddled inside, lips chattering.

"This should warm you up." Shay wrapped the child in the blanket then, after checking to be sure there were no animals inside the cave, sank down beside her and drew her close. "Better?"

"Yes." Maggie was silent for a few moments then she asked, "How long do we have to stay here?"

"I'm not sure." Shay had to be honest. "It's a big storm, honey. Listen." As if to emphasize her words, the wind chose that moment to send a shower of sand into the mouth of the cave. "But we're safe here." Shay didn't *feel* safe, but she would not let Maggie see her fear. "I brought the rest of the picnic for when you get hungry."

"Okay." Maggie peered through the gloom for several moments. When she finally spoke, her question surprised Shay. "Uncle Nick said your dad died. Did you have a good daddy?"

"I did, darling." Shay snuggled the girl close against her and bent her head to rest her cheek against Maggie's still-damp hair. "I had the best father a girl could want."

"So did I," whispered Maggie. She sniffled.

"I know." Though she tried to ignore the hiss of wind into the cave, worrisome what-ifs plagued Shay. "We were lucky to have had such good fathers," she said, struggling to blot out her unease.

Maggie frowned. "When I was in the hospital, a lady told me I was an orphan. I asked Grandma what that meant."

"What did Grandma say?"

"She said I wasn't an orphan because God's my daddy and Jesus is my brother." Maggie lifted her head. "And you know what else Grandma said?"

"Why don't you tell me, sweetheart?"

Shay's admiration for Mrs. Green's ability to teach her faith to her granddaughter was shattered by a strange noise. She leaned forward a little, concentrating on where the sound came from. Was it just the hiss of sand in the air as it hit the stones outside? Or an echo that kept rebounding inside?

Or was it something more sinister? They were near the front, but perhaps something had taken refuge in the back where she hadn't seen it. She shuddered at the thought.

Shay couldn't quiet her rising panic when a shadow on the cave wall moved. Her breath jammed in her chest. Every brain cell told her to grab Maggie and run.

God? The one-word prayer whispered straight from her heart to heaven.

Suddenly there was a lull in the wind. The whole world seemed to hush. Maggie's pure, confident tones rang out.

"Grandma said God isn't like other daddies. He knows how to take care of His kids." With that, Maggie closed her eyes and fell asleep.

I will never, never fail you nor forsake you.

This morning's verse bloomed crystal clear in Shay's head. The promise was hers. Maggie had accepted it. Now Shay could choose to believe it or she could fret and make herself sick with worry.

Either way, sooner or later, Nick would show up.

Because that's who he was.

Shay made her choice.

"I will trust You," she whispered. "We are safe in Your hands."

The wind raged again. The sand pelted the cave opening, and the sky was just as dark. But inside Shay's head, a reassuring presence blossomed, pushing out panic and fear.

Even if she never had her own family, she was part of God's family and He would never let her down.

Shay closed her eyes and worshipped. And in that moment she remembered a detail so startling, she knew it had to be from God.

"Shay? Shay!" Nick glared at the offending phone but no one answered. He dialed Shay's number but it went immediately to voice mail.

"What's wrong?" His mother hovered at his elbow.

"I'm not sure but I think they're in trouble, Mom." Nick met her gaze.

"Then you'll find them." Her confidence in him was reassuring.

"There was a lot of static. Nothing Shay said came through clearly. It sounded like she said they were at the moon." He shook his head, his hands fisted at his sides. "I'm pretty sure she also said her car was dead."

"The moon?" His mom frowned. "Is that some kind of amusement park?"

"Not that I know of." Why hadn't he gone along with them, or at least asked her to tell him where they were going? He glanced down at Hugs. The dog lay flopped on the floor at his feet, his big eyes fixed on Nick as if he knew something was wrong.

"If we don't know where to look, how can we find them?" Worry lines appeared at the corners of his mom's eyes.

"We'll get help." He dialed Kent. "Hey. Are you and Jaclyn okay?" He listened for a moment then explained the situation and what he thought he'd heard Shay say. "The thing is, I can't figure out what 'the moon' means."

"I haven't got a clue either. Hang on a sec." Kent talked to Jaclyn then returned. "Jaclyn says the Weather Channel is claiming this storm will let up in about an hour. I'll call Zac and Brianna. We'll head over to your place as soon as we can and go from there."

But go where?

"They're coming as soon as they can," Nick told his mother.

"But it will be dark soon, Nicky." The old nickname that his mother used only at the most stressful times told him how worried she was. "I'll pray."

"I hope that's enough to help Shay," he muttered.

"Prayer is always enough." His mom frowned. "If you say you trust God, you have to trust Him with everything, son. He has plans for Shay and Maggie. He isn't going to let harm come to them."

Worry chewed at Nick. This was exactly why he'd been so hesitant about that job in Seattle. What if this had happened when he was away? Who would be there for the ones he loved?

Loved?

Maggie, yes…but Shay, too?

The knowledge blindsided him, but he knew it was true. He did love Shay, and somewhere deep inside he'd known it for a while. So why hadn't he told her that when she said she loved him? Because he was afraid?

But fear was exactly why he wanted so desperately to see her healed, to see her happy, to look after her.

Because he was in love with her.

"Nick?"

"Yeah?" Half-dazed by this new understanding, he glanced at his mother.

"Why is it so hard for you to trust God? He's your Father."

"Sorry, but that analogy doesn't exactly inspire me, Mom." He let out a harsh laugh.

"God is nothing like your earthly father," she said. "But you're not just talking about God's trustworthiness, are you? You're also worried about your own."

"I am my father's son," Nick said bitterly. "I am just as bad at relationships as the old man was. I even walked out on a woman I said I loved," he admitted. "Twice. I can't be trusted with love."

"That's why this decision to take the job in Seattle is tearing you apart," she said. "You want to be here with Shay, but you won't take the risk."

"I love her." It felt good to finally say that aloud. "I want her to be happy. I want to *make* her happy. But I can't stay."

"Because?" his mother prodded.

"Because I don't think I will make her happy. Besides, the family needs me and I can't fail them. I can't fail you, or my sisters, or Maggie."

"Nick, you won't fail us no matter where you work. You've been there every time your sisters and I needed you." She touched his cheek. "Sometimes I think you've been there too much for us."

Nick gaped at her, stunned by her words, words that turned his entire perception of himself upside down.

"Your sisters and I all find it too easy to turn to you at the first hint of trouble, and like the dependable man you are, you rush in to rescue us." His mother smiled. "You always have, because you think no one else will. But that's a lie, Nick. God uses you when you let Him, yes. But God doesn't expect you to give up your life for us. If you're not available, He'll find some other way to see His will done."

Nick couldn't assimilate her words. For so long he'd been the go-to guy in his family. To just back off and let them deal with whatever—well, that just wasn't his way.

"You can't always be there for us, even though you want to be." She wrapped her arms around his waist and laid her head on his shoulder. "I am so immensely proud of you, Nick. You are everything a son should be and more. But you can't run yourself ragged trying to be all the things your father wasn't. You deserve to find happiness with Shay."

"But what if I fail Shay, like Dad failed you?" That memory of his father turning his back on his family still burned. "What if I mess up and hurt her?"

"Then you apologize and ask for forgiveness." She sighed. "Humans fail, dear. All of us. I failed your father, too." She smiled at his look of disbelief. "It's true."

"But Mom, if I stay in Hope, if I don't take that job—" Nick gulped. "What will I do?"

"I don't know, sweetheart. Take the time to woo the woman you love? Start thinking about what you want your own future to look like? Keep blessing people with your inventions?"

"You make it sound so simple."

"It is simple, Nicky." She leaned back. "Now, are you ready to pray with me?"

Nick thought of Shay and Maggie out there somewhere, alone and probably frightened. And then he thought of God wrapping His arms around Nick's loved ones, protecting them and keeping them safe, just as he wanted to.

Nick reached out and took his mother's hand as she led a prayer asking for the Father's guidance. Then Nick prayed his own prayer.

"God, You know how much I love Shay. But I can't keep her safe all the time. I trust You to bring Shay and Maggie home safely. I trust You to direct my future. Put me where You want me." He inhaled. "You know what the future holds, and You know how much I want a future with Shay. I leave it in Your hands, Father. Help us find Shay and Maggie. Please."

Nick lifted his head, met his mother's tearing eyes and smiled.

Now all they could do was wait for God to show them the next step.

Chapter Fourteen

Shay sat motionless with Maggie sleeping in her arms as the storm raged, waned and finally died away. The sky cleared, the wind calmed and the world around them returned to normal. She had just begun to nod off when she heard the pad of footsteps outside the cave.

Outlined by the moon, the shadow of an animal filled the cave opening. She couldn't tell exactly what it was. Only that it stood there, poised, waiting.

In that instant fear rose up like a tsunami and prepared to engulf Shay. Every muscle tensed. She wanted to scream but couldn't.

"The Lord is my shepherd, I shall not want." Maggie's soft but unfaltering voice surprised her, cutting through the cloud of fear.

As Maggie continued, the animal twisted its neck to watch them. Its eyes seemed to glow through the shadows, joining the host of stars behind it that glimmered and shone. On seeing those stars, Shay's fears melted away. God had created the stars and the animal and Maggie and her. Like a shepherd He led them all on the best path. Nothing happened that He wasn't in control of.

She joined Maggie, her voice growing more confident with every word.

"Even though I walk through the valley of the shadow of death, I fear no evil for thou art with me." Loudly, their voices raised in triumph, Shay and Maggie finished the verse. When Shay looked again, the animal was gone. All she could see now were stars. Laid out across the desert sky, they shone. Some were brighter, some were dimmer, but all of them shone, proclaiming the power and glory of God. Then, suddenly, a star burst out from the others and shot across the sky, scattering particles of light in a path behind it.

"Did you see that, Shay?"

"Yes, darling, I saw it," she said, remembering the night when she and Nick had watched the meteor shower. A powerful certainty filled her.

God had led her back to Hope, to Whispering Hope Clinic, and to Nick. He'd given the love she felt filling her heart. God would finish what He started.

"I can do that," she whispered.

"What?" Maggie asked.

"It's getting light. We should get our stuff together and be ready to leave. Your uncle will be here soon."

"Really?" Maggie's big brown eyes studied her.

"I'm positive." She grinned at the little girl. "Want to take a dip in the lake before he gets here?"

Maggie laughed and Shay laughed right along with her. God was in charge. He would take care of them. Always.

And that wasn't the only thing she held in her heart. She could hardly wait to tell Nick what she'd remembered. It could change everything—for both of them.

When Nick saw the red convertible, his heart jumped with relief. She was here.

He saw a picnic basket sitting on a ledge above him. As he

scrambled up toward it, he saw a cave behind it. He climbed quickly, using his hands to propel him faster.

"Shay? Maggie?" They weren't inside.

Nick moved back outside and dug out his cell phone to let everyone know he'd found the car. But he couldn't find cell service so he climbed a bit higher. And that's when he heard the singing.

His heart jumped for joy. Maggie's childish soprano accompanied by Shay's strong voice filled the hills and the valleys, echoing back to penetrate even the tiniest crevices.

"Our God is an awesome God," they sang.

"Yes, He is," Nick agreed, his heart skipping in time to the tune. "Thank You, God." He moved higher up the hill, anxious to hold his loved ones in his arms. He ducked through an overgrowth, and when he stepped free he saw Shay and Maggie seated at the edge of a small lake, legs dipping in and out of the water as they swayed together, arms around each other's waists. As far as Nick could tell, Shay looked perfectly calm, with no sign of panic marring her lovely face.

Thank You, Lord.

"Do you think that was loud enough for Uncle Nick to hear?" Maggie asked.

He stood silent, curious to hear Shay's response.

"Whether he heard it or not, Nick will find us. He won't let us down."

Such faith in him. For a moment the old worries besieged him, but he shoved them back and stepped forward. "You sure have a lot of faith in me," he said, his eyes meeting and holding Shay's.

"Yes." Shay gave him the most heart-stopping smile he had ever seen in his entire life.

"Oh, Uncle Nick, we had the awesome-est picnic." With Shay's helping hand, Maggie rose and walked over to encircle his legs with her arms.

"I don't think awesome-est is a word," he said with a chuckle, swinging her into his arms.

"It is when you're talking about Shay's picnics. We missed you." She hugged his neck then leaned back to look into his face. "You should come next time, Uncle Nick."

"I intend to, Maggie-mine. I intend to be at every one of Shay's picnics in the future." He set his niece down and locked his gaze on Shay. "If she'll let me."

"Every time you're home, you mean?" Shay swung her feet out of the water and rose. She tilted her head to one side, watching as he smiled.

"I am home." Nick waited for her to get closer, and when she did he reached out and pulled her into his arms, burying his face in her hair. "This is my home, Shay. With you." He leaned back just a little, so he could see her face. "I love you. I want a future with you."

"But—" She stopped, though her arms were already winding around his neck. "What about your job?"

"They'll have to find someone else. My life is here in Hope." It felt so good to say that. "I love you, Shay. Will you marry me and share whatever future God gives us together?"

"Say yes, Shay," Maggie chanted, her dark eyes shining.

"Yes," Shay repeated. "I love you, Nick."

Nick didn't need anything else. He pulled the gorgeous Shay Parker as close as he could and kissed her. He poured everything into that kiss—his worry about her and Maggie, his relief that God had answered his prayers in a way he'd never expected, and his dream of a future with the most beautiful woman he'd ever known. He would have kept on kissing her but a small hand tugged so hard on his pant leg, it broke his concentration.

"Excuse me a minute—don't go anywhere," he said to Shay. He peered down at his grinning niece. "What?"

"Are you and Shay going to get married?" Maggie asked.

Nick looked at Shay. She smiled at him. "Yes," they said together.

"Can I be in it? I'd practice ever so hard to carry the rings or whatever you want. I promise I wouldn't mess up or…"

Shay eased out of Nick's arms and hunched down to lay a finger over Maggie's lips to stop her words. Then she drew the girl close.

"Maggie, my darling Maggie," Shay said. "Do you think Nick and I would even think about getting married without you?"

"I don't know," came Maggie's muffled response.

Shay turned to smile at him, and Nick's knees turned to mush. Lord, he loved this woman. He squatted down beside them and folded them both into his embrace.

"You're the one who brought Shay and me together in the first place. You're the one who taught us to trust God. We watched your faith and we learned how to trust Him." He smiled at her. "You have to be in our wedding, Maggie-mine."

Maggie beamed. "Good. Can I wear a pink dress? I love pink."

"You can wear whatever you want, sweetheart," his wife-to-be said. "Maybe Uncle Nick will wear a matching pink tie."

"Pink? Shay, come on." He straightened, ready to plead his case.

"And we could get a big pink ribbon for Hugs," Maggie agreed. "He has to be part of the wedding, too."

"No. Absolutely not. That dog is a—" Nick stopped short. His two ladies were looking at him as if he'd doused them with water from the lake. His heart melted. "So, is this what it's going to be like?" he asked meekly.

Shay grinned. "Want to back out?"

"Not on your life." He held out a hand, pulled her up-right and pressed another kiss on her mouth. "We are getting married, pink ties and dogs and bows notwithstanding. You hear me?"

"I hear you, Nick. I can hardly wait." Shay wrapped her arms around him and kissed him back with a fervor that drew no complaints from Nick.

He checked his heart and felt only anticipation about their future and what God would show them.

"Not that kissing again," Maggie grumbled. "I want some breakfast."

Nick burst out laughing. "Okay, Mags, we'll go get breakfast." He took her hand and helped her down the path, glancing at Shay, delighted to see the same joy reflected on her face that warmed his insides. "But if you're going to be in our wedding, I've got a condition."

"What condition?" Maggie planted her hands on her hips.

"I get to kiss Shay whenever I want and you don't get to complain about it." He set her inside his truck and fastened her seat belt. Then he held out his hand. "Deal?"

With a heavy sigh, Maggie shook his hand. "Deal," she agreed.

"Good. Now sit tight for a minute, will you?" He closed the truck door then turned to face his best friend. "I don't know how this will turn out," he said. "I have a verbal contract with the team. I might have to go back and work a couple of months until they find someone else."

"God will work something out," she said, her lovely face glowing. "However He does it, we'll keep trusting Him to lead us."

"Sounds good to me." Conscious of Maggie's peering eyes, Nick contented himself with one last quick kiss.

"Nick, I remembered something important last night." She took a deep breath. "I know who the stalker is. I remembered him talking to the maintenance man one time, and the man called him 'son.'" She smiled at his quick intake of breath. "It should be enough for the police to catch him, shouldn't it?"

"It should be more than enough, sweet Shay." Nick hugged her. "Are you okay?"

"Yes, thank God. I am very okay." She hugged him hard. "Let's get on with the rest of our lives."

"Deal." He helped Shay into his truck and drove to his mother's house, where Maggie, after wiggling out of her grandmother's arms, broke the news about their upcoming wedding.

"I'm so delighted." His mom hugged him then embraced Shay. "You've always been a daughter of my heart. This will make it reality." She stopped. "How was it up there? I remember you told me you had a fear of the desert at night."

"I gave all my fears to God," Shay explained. "I don't know what He has planned for my future, but with Him by my side, and Nick," she added, grasping his hand, "I know I can do anything He sets before me."

"That's quite a lesson."

Shay gave Mrs. Green a smile. "I learned it from someone very special, and very wise."

A few minutes later Jaclyn, Kent, Brianna and Zac arrived while Shay was on the phone with the NYPD. Once her friends had heard the story of the cave ordeal and her returned memory, Shay told them she and Nick were getting married. After a lot of hugging and congratulations, the ladies tipped their heads together and began wedding planning. Nick led the men out to the deck, where they sat drinking his mom's lemonade.

"So what will you do in Hope?" Zac finally asked the question Nick figured was on everyone's mind.

"I have no idea. Odd jobs, maybe." Nick shrugged, pretending it didn't matter. "I'll do something. The important thing is that I stay here."

The other two men were silent for several moments. Finally Kent spoke, scuffing his toe against the deck as he said the words slowly. "I think the Lord's got more in store for you than odd jobs. I think He brought you back here for a reason." He slapped Nick on the back. "Just hang in there. He'll show you His plan soon enough."

Nick opened his mouth to respond but a squeal from inside had the three men jumping out of their seats.

Brianna stuck her head out the screen door.

"Kent, you need to get your wife to the hospital. Apparently she's been having contractions for a while but didn't want to interrupt the search. Well?" she demanded, hands on her hips. "Why are the three of you staring at me like that? A baby's coming."

"Baby. Right. Hospital." Kent jumped up and stalked toward the truck—without his wife.

Nick started laughing. "You hold him there," he told Zac. "I'll go help Jaclyn. We'd better follow them in. I have a hunch he's going to need us before this day is over."

"What are friends for?" Zac high-fived him. "Congratulations, by the way. You and Shay are perfect for each other."

"Perfectly matched," Jaclyn agreed as she stepped onto the deck. Then she groaned and grabbed her friends' hands. "Oh, boy." She puffed through the contraction with Brianna's coaching, then muttered, "I need to leave. Now."

"You think?" Nick said as Kent roared up, lifted his wife into the truck and roared away.

"Keep praying, Mom," Nick whispered in her ear as he hugged her. "This is a turning out to be a day when we need a lot of God's help."

"All we have to do is ask." She nudged him. "Now, take Shay to the hospital. Maggie and I will work on the wedding. We know exactly what we want, don't we, honey?"

"Pink," Maggie said with a nod. "Lots and lots of pink. It's Shay's favorite color."

"I see." His stomach clenched at the thought of what the two of them would create, but he tamped down his misgivings, helped Shay into his truck and followed the others.

"Is your favorite color really pink?"

"No." She laughed. "But it really doesn't matter, does it? I just want to marry you."

He picked up her hand and kissed her palm.

"Now, that's what I call having your priorities sorted," Nick told her. "Because I want to marry you, too. And soon. As soon as possible." He turned to look into her beautiful face. "What do you know about women having babies?"

"Not a thing, but I guess we'll trust God to teach us something new."

For the first time in a long time, trusting God sounded absolutely perfect to Nick.

Epilogue

"I can't believe a world-class designer just gave you this wedding dress. It's spectacular." Jaclyn sat on the living-room sofa holding her sleeping daughter, Lily Grace. Liam Kent lay nearby, wide awake but quiet in the blanket Shay had made.

"Evan is a dear friend and an amazing designer. I love his work. His dresses have always made me feel as if I'm a princess. This one certainly does." Shay smoothed a hand over the feather-light silk creation, a one-of-a-kind design made especially for her, more beautiful than anything she'd ever worn.

"I can't believe you look more lovely today than you ever did on any magazine cover," Brianna said as she watched Shay bend to press a tender kiss on each baby's cheek.

"Well, thank you, Jaclyn. But what *I* can't believe is how a doctor can be pregnant with twins and not know it! You always were an overachiever, Jaclyn."

Jaclyn grinned as Shay and Brianna admired the babies.

"Those things are all true, of course. And wonderful besides. You girls are right to notice them. But what I can't believe is that the New York police finally caught Shay's stalker." Mrs. Green shook her head. "That memory she had in the cave with Maggie was certainly God timing, wasn't it?" She asked Shay to give them more details.

"Dom was the son of the building maintenance guy. He was supposed to be helping his dad but he'd often disappear for hours at a time. His father thought he was playing video games or something since it had been happening for years." It didn't bother Shay at all to talk about it. "Maybe that was true when he was younger, but when the modeling agency bought the building as a shoot site because of its roof terrace, Dom apparently became mesmerized by the models. Of course he had access to everything and he'd keep the pink telephone message cards we threw away. He started spying on us and got fixated on me."

"Who wouldn't?" Jaclyn asked with a proud smile.

"Nick said he started by stealing some of the jewelry you were modeling," Mrs. Green said.

"Yes, but his dad found out and put it back. He never knew Dom was following me or threatening me. And that only started because Dom saw me give away some flowers he'd sent. Though I didn't realize that."

"I'm just glad they got him. That Dom would have gone on deceiving women and terrorizing them if you hadn't remembered who he was and given the police enough information that they set a trap that he couldn't get out of. Now, thank God, he won't hurt anyone again." Mrs. Green reached out to brush Shay's cheek with her hand, a fond smile lighting her face. "God answers. He always answers."

"Yes, He does," Brianna agreed. She checked her watch. "Hey, we've got to get this woman to the church on time. Let's move it. Where's her veil?"

"Where are the flowers?" Jaclyn asked.

"Where's my phone?" Shay said as the familiar peal sounded. She found it and saw Nick's number. "I have to take this," she said. "It's my groom." Her heart swelled with joy as she said his name. "Nick?"

"Hey, gorgeous. Why aren't you at the church? I'm waiting."

"I'm on my way. Be patient," she said. "After today we'll have forever."

"Yes, we will. Listen, God really came through for us, sweetheart." Nick sounded ecstatic.

"What's going on?" Surely nothing would go wrong now— no. *Trust God,* Shay ordered herself. He didn't bring you this far to leave you. "You sound excited, Nick."

"I am. We just received the most perfect wedding gift."

"You opened it without me?" Shay asked.

"I was told to. It was a letter. You won't believe this, Shay. Thanks to a little push from Chief Burger, the town of Hope just offered me the job of activities director," he told her, his voice jubilant.

Shay closed her eyes, her heart exploding with praise. "Go on."

"They said that while I was in Seattle working out my notice to the team, they realized there were so many groups that had worked with me that they needed someone on staff to keep them running. I am employed full-time starting the first of next month."

"Praise God," she whispered, trying not to cry and ruin her makeup.

"You'd better double that praise, sweetheart." His excitement transmitted clearly over the phone. "Because they've also initiated a fund to create that wellness center you and I proposed. They believe it will benefit the whole town and are anxious to get together with us as soon as we return from our honeymoon to hammer out details!"

"Fantastic!" Shay couldn't help but whisper a prayer of thanks.

"I love you, Shay Parker."

"That's soon-to-be Mrs. Green, to you, buddy. And I love

you, too, Nick." The enormity of the love that filled her heart and soul swamped Shay.

"Uh-oh. Maggie just texted me." Nick chuckled. "She wants me to get my boutonniere. Now."

"You'd better obey our 'wedding planner.' I'll follow shortly," Shay promised.

"And then we'll begin our future," he murmured. "I can hardly wait."

"Me, either." Shay saw her friends gesturing at the clock. "I love you. Bye."

"The flowers are at the church," Mrs. Green said, emerging from the bedroom. "Someone put them in the fridge in the basement. That's why we couldn't find them. We're good to—oh, Shay. You look so very happy."

"Because I am." She explained about Nick's new job. "Thank you all," she said, studying each dear face. "You've made this the most wonderful day of my life."

"Well, us and Nick," Brianna teased.

"Yes, especially Nick," she agreed.

Jaclyn looked at her watch. "We're behind schedule. Is Kent here?"

"Outside with the limo," Mrs. Green confirmed. "Give me one of those babies to carry, Jaclyn. Brianna, you help Shay. We don't want the bride to be late for her own wedding."

They arrived at the church and were escorted into the bride's dressing room by a very excited Maggie, who looked sweet in a pink sundress that Shay had picked out for her. She held Shay's bouquet and a small rectangular box.

"This is for you, Shay," she said holding out the silver box. "With lots of love from Uncle Nick."

"Oh." Shay lifted the lid and found a silver filigree necklace with a tiny heart nestled inside. In the center of the heart sparkled an emerald.

"It's lovely," Mrs. Green said. "Shall I put it on for you?"

"Yes, please." Shay leaned over while the necklace was fastened. Then she drew out a tiny card that said, You have my heart, Shay. Always. Love, Nick. "It's the perfect wedding gift," she whispered, eager to tell him thanks in a more personal way.

"Here, Shay!" Maggie said, holding out a sheaf of dark pink sweetheart roses. "These are from Uncle Nick, too. He chose them from Grandma's garden."

"They're lovely." Shay sniffed. She glanced around, overcome by the generosity of everyone who'd helped make her wedding happen in such a short time.

"I just wish we could have finished renovations on the church before your wedding," Jaclyn said, tracing a finger across the worn paneling on the wall.

"I don't think we'll ever be done with that," Brianna said. "We'll probably still be working on it when all of our kids graduate from college and come back to Hope to be married. That's how it should be, isn't it? The church growing and changing as our lives do?"

"I like the sound of that," Shay murmured as she set her veil in place.

"Brianna and I wanted to give you a special gift, because you're our best friend and because we're glad you joined us in the clinic, and because we're so happy you and Nick are getting married." Jaclyn grinned.

"Yes." Brianna smiled at Jaclyn. "We wanted something really special and something lasting. So we're going to make a special donation to the wellness center you and Nick put forward. It will be funding earmarked for a children's section so that no child who uses it will ever pay a fee."

"I can't imagine a better gift," Shay said, embracing the pair. Of course she was crying. Of course it took a few moments to repair the damage. But her joy was so great that nothing could dim it.

"Shay, Uncle Nick is waiting at the front," Maggie said after she'd peeked out the door. "The church is full and everyone's ready." She clutched the door. "Can we start now?"

"Yes. We can start now." Shay nodded. Maggie opened the door wide. They all walked to the back of the church. "Thank you for making our day so special," Shay whispered to Maggie. The little girl started down the aisle first, walking proudly with no limp. Shay's heart gave a bump of pride. God had certainly brought her to this place—Maggie was confirmation of that. Brianna followed in a lighter pink press, then Jaclyn in the palest pink of all. Both of them stood next to their husbands, Nick's best men. The organ sounded and the congregation rose. Shay fixed her eyes on Nick.

Shay spared a thought for her father. He'd have been so proud to walk her down the aisle. She missed him desperately, but she knew he was watching.

She focused on Nick until she was finally by his side. His gaze held hers as Brianna and Jaclyn, Kent and Zac linked their hands together. Cherished and protected in his grip, Shay listened as he recited the age-old words that would bind them as husband and wife before God for the rest of their lives. Nick said his vows slowly, his eyes locked with hers, his voice quiet, the promise meant for her ears alone. He didn't stumble over the words as he'd teased he would. And when he slid the ring on her finger, it was as if her heart locked with his.

Then it was her turn. Nothing had ever felt more right than this moment.

"I, Shay, take you, Nick to be my lawfully wedded husband. For better, for worse, for richer, for poorer, in sickness and in health. As long as we both shall live."

After a short homily on what marriage meant, Pastor Marty told Nick he could kiss his bride. As his lips covered hers, Shay knew she was finally at home.

It was when they moved to sign the register that Shay saw

it—a spray of the tiniest pure white roses in a silver vase on the table. While Nick was signing she leaned forward and peeked at the card tucked in with a pink ribbon.

To Shay, with love, Jessica.

"What's wrong?" Nick whispered as Shay gasped.

"Everything is right. An old friend of ours sent her blessing." She showed him the roses. "Everything's perfect."

When the ceremony was over, the pastor announced, "Ladies and gentlemen, may I present Mr. and Mrs. Nick Green."

The congregation clapped as they walked together down the aisle. Outside the church, they formed a receiving line with bubbles filling the air around them, sparkling iridescence in the summer sunshine.

The reception was held under a huge white tent as the sun dipped behind the mountains. Tiny paper lanterns strung all over the ceiling were switched on as everyone found their place. Anyone who wanted to come had been invited to celebrate and that's exactly what they did, toasting the beautiful bride and her handsome groom. There was much tinkling of glasses to encourage the couple's kisses. Then Shay threw her bouquet which Mrs. Green caught. Finally Shay and Nick cut the wedding cake Susan Swan had made and passed it out to their guests.

It was while her friends were helping her change out of her wedding dress that Shay's friend Jaclyn asked, "Any idea where Nick's taking you for your honeymoon?"

"New York." Shay smiled at her two friends' dismayed looks.

"Why?" Brianna asked.

"It's time for us to make new memories in that city. It's only the beginning of what God has in store for us." Shay hugged them both then walked out the door and tucked her arm into Nick's, delighted to know that God had given her such a wonderful gift of love out of such a terrible time.

When everyone had wished them well and they were on their way out of town in her convertible, Shay took a moment to look at the man by her side—her husband.

"Do we have time for a side trip before we catch the plane?" she asked. Nick frowned but nodded. "We need to stop by my place."

"We've got a pretty tight schedule," he said, but he drove there quickly, casting her questioning looks but remaining silent until they arrived. Then his eyes widened. When he looked at her, he seemed stunned.

"You gave me the most lovely wedding gift," she said, fingering the chain at her neck. "This is mine to you. With all my love."

Nick caught her close and kissed her. Shay laughed at his quick glance over her shoulder.

"Go and check it out quickly," she said. "Then we have to go."

"Yes, ma'am." Nick vaulted over the side of her car and raced toward the building she'd had moved onto the property last night. He dragged open the door and peered inside. A moment later his woohoo echoed across the desert.

Shay sat content, unable to suppress her smile as she waited. After a few minutes Nick came racing out of the building, yanked open her door and caught her in his arms, swinging her around and around.

"I take it you like it," she said with a laugh, twining her arms around his neck. "I hope you enjoy your new shop, my darling husband. I know you'll use it to help those who need you. Those God sends your way."

"I love you, wife," he whispered. "And not because you gave me the most wonderful inventing shop in the world. You are the most beautiful woman I've ever known and your beauty starts in your heart. I love you." He kissed her, pouring his heart and all of his feelings into that kiss.

And Shay kissed him back until Nick finally drew away, set her in the car and took his place behind the wheel. But before he drove away he cupped her chin in his palms.

"From here on it's you and me and God. I love you, Shay."

"I love you, too, Nick." She leaned her head against his shoulder as they drove into the sunset.

Sometimes the unscripted moments when you let go of the controls and just trusted were the best of your life.

* * * * *

Dear Reader:

I hope you've enjoyed *Perfectly Matched,* the last installment of my HEALING HEARTS series. Best friends Nick and Shay just needed a little time and the touch of God's healing hand for love to blossom between them. Each had to learn that trust in God means believing He is there and cares for you, no matter what happens around you.

Thank you for spending this time with me. I love hearing from readers. You can contact me via email at loisricher@yahoo.com, through my website at www.loisricher.com or like me on Facebook. If you'd prefer to write, please do send me note by snail mail to Box 639, Nipawin, Sask. Canada S0E 1E0, and I'll respond as quickly as I can.

Until we meet again I wish you His peace, the kind that passes all understanding, His joy, which never disappears, and the sweet solace of His everlasting love.

Blessings,

Questions for Discussion

1. Shay's stalker left her insecure and uncertain about her safety and her future. Discuss issues in your own life that have made you feel alone and vulnerable and distant from God.

2. As an eleven-year-old boy, Nick was profoundly affected by his father's decision to abandon his family and by the gossip he overheard. He assumed responsibility for his sisters and his mother. Consider ways parents and the community in general can help children feel secure and loved in the face of their parents' marital issues.

3. Maggie's faith in God's love for her is unwavering despite her injuries. It's this faith that both Nick and Shay lack in themselves. List reasons why children seem to find it so much easier to trust God. Are there ways adults can emulate a child's faith?

4. Even years later, Shay couldn't shake the legacy her stalker had left her with. Discuss experiences that have affected your world so deeply you now find it hard to forget them. Do you feel your faith has affected the afterthoughts of these experiences?

5. To most people, except her closest friends, Shay seemed to lead a perfectly normal life. Take time to think about your circle of friends and family. Are there those who seem fine on the surface but about whom you've noticed something unusual? Did you pause in your busy day to talk to them, or do you feel that's prying and that they'd

do better to handle their issues alone? When it is okay to push past the platitudes and try to help another?

6. In the story, Nick's mother became Shay's mentor. This woman's experience of God's love after her husband's abandonment taught her that God doesn't always remove problems but sometimes uses them to teach His children. Consider some tough issues you've faced in your own life and whether God used them to teach you and, through them, build your faith.

7. Nick took Shay to watch a meteor shower, hoping to help her overcome a longstanding fear of the desert at night, but he was challenged himself. Explore your view of God and what you believe is true of His nature. Is there a biblical basis for your beliefs, or are they the result of what you've been told or of a life experience?

8. *Perfectly Matched* is primarily a story about family. Reflect on your own family and the impact they've had on your life or the lack of impact if you don't have a family. Ponder the difference a strong, supportive network can make in a child's life and opportunities you might have to provide such a support network for a child who doesn't have one.

9. Shay made a deliberate decision to trust God, used Nick's mom as a mentor and modeled Maggie's faith as she struggled to overcome the legacy of fear her stalker had left. Discuss alternate ways she could have fought her fear.

10. Shay unveiled a repressed memory of the stalker while she was in the cave with Maggie. Offer suggestions as to why God allows some things in our pasts to stay buried.

11. In the end, Nick chose to give up the security of his football job in order to stay in Hope, to be near his family and wait for God to show him the next step. Was this a foolhardy choice? What would you have done?

12. Fear and trust are the main issues in this book. How do they manifest in your life? How do you combat them?

COMING NEXT MONTH from Love Inspired®
AVAILABLE MARCH 19, 2013

THE COWBOY LAWMAN
Cooper Creek
Brenda Minton
DEA agent Mia Cooper returns home to heal from an injury. Will she have a chance to restore her health and her heart in the arms of childhood friend Slade McKennon?

MAKING HIS WAY HOME
Mirror Lake
Kathryn Springer
Home to sell his grandfather's house, Cole Merrick comes face-to-face with Grace Eversea—and the sweet summer romance that they've never forgotten.

GEORGIA SWEETHEARTS
Missy Tippens
Forced to share the same store, Lilly Barnes and Daniel Foreman clash from the get-go. What will it take for them to learn that sometimes opposites really do attract?

MENDING THE DOCTOR'S HEART
Tina Radcliffe
When doctors Ben Rogers and Sara Elliott compete to win a job at a medical clinic, can they put their troubled pasts behind them and follow their hearts?

THE RANCHER NEXT DOOR
Betsy St. Amant
When firefighter Caley Foster moves next door to handsome rancher Brady McCollough, nothing prepares her for *these* kinds of sparks!

REKINDLED ROMANCE
Lorraine Beatty
Back home to regain her health, Shelby Russell finds herself babysitting for Matt Durrant's adorable kids. Trouble is, he's the same man Shelby jilted for her career years ago.

Look for these and other Love Inspired books wherever books are sold, including most bookstores, supermarkets, discount stores and drugstores.

LICNM0313

REQUEST YOUR FREE BOOKS!

2 FREE INSPIRATIONAL NOVELS
PLUS 2
FREE
MYSTERY GIFTS

Love Inspired®

LII3

SPECIAL EXCERPT FROM

Love Inspired HISTORICAL

When a tragedy brings a group of orphans to a small
Nebraska town, shy schoolteacher Holly Sanders is
determined to find the children homes...and soften dour
sheriff Mason Wright's heart, along the way!
Read on for a sneak preview of

FAMILY LESSONS by Allie Pleiter,
the first in the ORPHAN TRAIN series.

"You saved us," Holly said, as she moved toward
Sheriff Wright.

He looked at her, his blue eyes brittle and hollow. She so
rarely viewed those eyes—downcast as they often were or
hidden in the shadow of his hat brim. "No."

"But it is true." Mason Wright was the kind of man who
would take Arlington's loss as a personal failure, ignoring
all the lives—including hers—he had just saved, and she
hated that. Hated that she'd fail in this attempt just as she
failed in *every* attempt to make him see his worth.

He held her gaze just then. "No," he repeated, but only a
little softer. Then his attention spread out beyond her to take
in the larger crisis at hand.

"Is she the other agent?" He nodded toward Rebecca
Sterling and the upset children, now surrounded by the few
other railcar passengers. "Liam mentioned a Miss..."

"Sterling, yes, that's her. Liam!" Holly suddenly remembered the brave orphan boy who'd run off to get help. "Is
Liam all right?"

"Shaken, but fine. Clever boy."

"I was so worried, sending him off."

He looked at her again, this time with something she could almost fool herself into thinking was admiration. "It was quick and clever. If anyone saved the day here, it was you."

Holly blinked. From Mason Wright, that was akin to a complimentary gush. "It was the only thing I could think of to do."

A child's cry turned them both toward the bedlam surrounding Miss Sterling. The children were understandably out of control with fear and shock, and Miss Sterling didn't seem to be in any shape to take things in hand. Who would be in such a situation?

She would, that's who. Holly was an excellent teacher with a full bag of tricks at her disposal to wrangle unruly children. With one more deep breath, she strode off to save the day a second time.

Don't miss FAMILY LESSONS
by Allie Pleiter, available April 2013
from Love Inspired Historical.

Man to trust…and love?
A love worth fighting for?
She'd never needed anyone…until now

When Slade McKennon comes looking for Mia Cooper, the
Dawson sheriff's only mission is to keep her safe. But the
wounded DEA agent isn't ready to trust the man whose past
is so inextricably entwined with hers. Slade lives by his own
code of honor—one that prevents the widowed single father
from pursuing the woman he's known most of his life. Still,
it's hard to fight the powerful attraction that's drawing them
closer together. As danger once again stalks Mia, Slade can't
let their complicated history keep her from the only place she
belongs—with *him*—cherished and protected in his arms.

The Cowboy Lawman

by

Brenda Minton

www.LoveInspiredBooks.com

LI87805

Love Inspired HISTORICAL

In the fan-favorite miniseries
Amish Brides of Celery Fields

ANNA SCHMIDT

presents

Second Chance Proposal

The sweetest homecoming.
He came home…for her.
A love rekindled.

Lydia Goodloe hasn't forgotten a single thing about John Amman—including the way he broke her heart eight years ago. Since John left Celery Fields to make his fortune, Lydia has devoted herself to teaching. John risked becoming an outcast to give Lydia everything she deserved. He couldn't see that what she really wanted was a simple life—with him. Lydia is no longer the girl he knew. Now she's the woman who can help him reclaim their long-ago dream of home and family…if he can only win her trust once more.

Amish Brides

CELERY FIELDS

Love awaits these Amish women.

www.LoveInspiredBooks.com
LIH82959